A magical evening shattered
in an instant . . .

On Friday, Chandler drove up to take me to the movies. He was wearing a black mock turtleneck shirt, which brought out the dark color in his eyes. I thought he looked very sexy, and practically leaped into the car to sit beside him. I couldn't remember when I had been happier.

As we started away, Grandad came out of nowhere onto the driveway and stood in the wash of Chandler's car headlights. His gray hair looked like it was on fire, his eyes blazing at us. Chandler hit the brake pedal and I gasped. Suddenly, Grandad raised his right hand, and I saw he was holding his sacred old Bible. He held it up like some potential victim of a vampire would hold up a cross in a horror movie, and then he stepped to the side and disappeared into the shadows.

Chandler turned to me, amazed. "What was that all about?"

"Just drive," I said, choking back my tears. Chandler stared at me. "Drive, Chandler, please."

HONEY

V.C. Andrews® Books

The Dollanganger Family Series
Flowers in the Attic
Petals on the Wind
If There Be Thorns
Seeds of Yesterday
Garden of Shadows

The Casteel Family Series
Heaven
Dark Angel
Fallen Hearts
Gates of Paradise
Web of Dreams

The Cutler Family Series
Dawn
Secrets of the Morning
Twilight's Child
Midnight Whispers
Darkest Hour

The Landry Family Series
Ruby
Pearl in the Mist
All That Glitters
Hidden Jewel
Tarnished Gold

The Logan Family Series
Melody
Heart Song
Unfinished Symphony
Music in the Night
Olivia

The Orphans Miniseries
Butterfly
Crystal
Brooke
Raven
Runaways (full-length novel)

The Wildflowers Miniseries
Misty
Star
Jade
Cat
Into the Garden (full-length novel)

The Hudson Family Series
Rain
Lightning Strikes
Eye of the Storm
The End of the Rainbow

The Shooting Stars Series
Cinnamon
Ice
Rose
Honey

My Sweet Audrina
(does not belong to a series)

Published by POCKET BOOKS

V.C. ANDREWS®

Honey

POCKET BOOKS

New York   London   Toronto   Sydney   Singapore

Following the death of Virginia Andrews, the Andrews family worked with a carefully selected writer to organize and complete Virginia Andrews' stories and to create additional novels, of which this is one, inspired by her storytelling genius.

This book is a work of fiction. Names, characters, places and incidents are products of the author's imagination or are used fictitiously. Any resemblance to actual events or locales or persons, living or dead, is entirely coincidental.

An *Original* Publication of POCKET BOOKS

POCKET BOOKS, a division of Simon & Schuster, Inc.
1230 Avenue of the Americas, New York, NY 10020

Copyright © 2001 by the Vanda General Partnership

ISBN: 0-671-03996-2

First Pocket Books paperback printing October 2001

10 9 8 7 6 5 4 3 2 1

V.C. ANDREWS and VIRGINIA ANDREWS are registered trademarks of the Vanda General Partnership.

POCKET and colophon are registered trademarks of Simon & Schuster, Inc.

For information regarding special discounts for bulk purchases, please contact Simon & Schuster Special Sales at 1-800-456-6798 or business@simonandschuster.com

Front cover illustration by Lisa Falkenstern

Printed in the U.S.A.

Honey

Prologue

—◊—

During the spring of my seventeenth year, I learned a shocking truth about my family. It turned my blood so cold, I thought I would freeze in place, become a statue like Lot's wife in the Bible.

Neither my mother nor my father wanted me to ever know that there were such dark secrets buried in our family vaults, secrets that deserved to be buried forever and ever.

Daddy once said, "As soon as we're born, we're given private burdens to carry, burdens we simply inherit. Sometimes those are the burdens no one but you can carry for yourself, no matter how much someone loves you and cherishes you, Honey.

"In fact, the truth is, the more you love someone, the more you want to keep him or her from ever knowing the deepest, darkest secrets in your heart."

"Why, Daddy?" I asked.

He smiled.

"We all want to be perfect for the one we love."

That meant no stains, no dark evil, nothing that would bring shame and disgrace along with my name. I knew that.

I also would soon know why it was impossible.

1

—❦—

Never Say Good-bye

In the spring of my senior year in high school, my uncle Peter was killed when his airplane crashed in the field he was crop dusting. A witness said the engine just choked and died on him. He was only thirty-five years old, and he had been my first pretend boyfriend. He had taken me flying at least a dozen times in his plane, each time more fun and exciting than the time before. When he performed his aerial acrobatics with me in the passenger seat beside him, I screamed at the top of my lungs. I screamed with a smile on my face, the way most people do when they have just gone over a particularly steep peak of tracks on the roller coaster at the Castle Rock Fun Park, which was only a few miles east of Columbus. Uncle Peter had taken me there, too.

He was my father's younger brother, but the five years between them seemed like a gap of centuries when it came to comparing their personalities. Daddy was often almost as serious and religious as Grandad Forman. Both were what anyone would call workaholics on our corn farm, actually Grandad's five-hundred-acre corn farm, which also had chickens and cows, mainly for our own consumption of eggs and milk. Grandad sold the remainder to some local markets.

Everything still belonged to Grandad, which was something he never let any of us forget, especially my step-uncle Simon, who lived in a makeshift room over the cow barn. Grandad Forman claimed that way Simon would be close to his work. One of his chores every day was milking and caring for the milk cows. He was the son of Grandad's first wife, Tess, who had lost her first husband, Clayton, when his truck turned over on the interstate and was hit by a tractor trailer. Clayton worked for Grandad at the time.

Simon had just been born when Tess married Grandad, but Grandad always regarded him as if he were an illegitimate child, working him hard and treating him like he was outside the family, treating him like the village idiot.

There were only very rare times when all of us,

my uncle Peter, my father and mother, and my step-uncle Simon would be around Grandad's dark oak dining room table, reciting grace and enjoying a meal and an evening together. However, when we were, it was easy to see the vast differences among everyone.

Mommy was tall with a shapely figure, often kept well-hidden under her loosely fitted garments. She didn't wear any makeup and never went to a beauty parlor. Her rich, dark brown hair was usually kept pinned up. On special occasions, I helped her wave a French knot. Mommy wasn't born here. She had come from Russia when she was in her late teen years, accompanied by her aunt, Ethel, who was a relative of Grandad Forman's through marriage.

Simon was the biggest of the men in our family. His father had been a very big man, six foot five and nearly three hundred pounds. Simon had grown very quickly—too quickly, according to Grandad Forman, who claimed Uncle Simon's body drained too much from his brain in the process. Always taller than any-one his age, Simon was large, towering, and lanky, awkward for almost anything but heavy manual labor, which only made him more massive and stronger. When I was very little, I rode on his shoulders, clutching his hair like the reins of a horse.

Simon never did well in school. Grandad claimed the teachers told him Simon was barely a shade or two above mentally retarded. I never believed that to be true. I knew in my heart he simply would rather be outside and couldn't keep his eyes from the classroom windows, mesmerized by the flight of a bird or even the mad circling of insects.

Simon was only twelve when Grandad Forman moved him into the barn and more or less forced him to leave public school. Besides his farm chores, Simon's only other real interest was his beautiful flower garden. Even Grandad Forman was forced to admit Simon had a magical green thumb when it came to nourishing the beauty he could garner from a seed. My mother and I were often the happy recipients of a mixed bouquet of redolent fresh flowers, to place in vases in our rooms or throughout the house. It amazed both of us how something so delicate could come from someone so hulking.

Anyone would look small beside Simon, but Uncle Peter was barely five foot nine and slim to the verge of being called thin. He had as big an appetite as my daddy or even as Simon at times, but he was always moving, joking, singing, or dancing. His body tossed off fattening foods and weight like someone tossing heavy items out of a boat to keep it from sinking. He had long, flaxen hair, green eyes, and a smile that could beam good feelings across our biggest cornfield. He cheered up everyone he met, excluding Grandad, who ordinarily viewed a smile and a laugh as a possible crack in the spiritual wall that kept the devil at bay.

Sometimes, for fun at dinner—when Uncle Simon was permitted to eat with us—Uncle Peter would challenge him to an arm wrestle and put his graceful, almost feminine fingers into the cavern of Uncle Simon's bear-claw palm. Uncle Simon would smile at Uncle Peter's great effort to move his arm back a tenth of an inch. Once, he even put both his hands in one of Uncle Simon's and then he got up and threw his whole body into the effort, while Uncle Simon sat there as unmoving as a giant boulder, staring up at him in wonder the way an elephant might wonder at a mouse trying to push it away. Daddy and Mommy laughed. Grandad Forman called him an idiot and ordered them both to stop their tomfoolery at his dinner table, but not as gruffly as he ordered me or Daddy or even Mommy when he wanted us to perform some chore or obey some command.

I always felt Grandad Forman was less severe on Uncle Peter. If Grandad had any soft or kind bones in his body, he turned them only on him, favoring him as much or as best he could favor anyone. From the pictures I saw of her, Uncle Peter did look more like his mother than he did Grandad, and I wondered if that was what Grandad saw in him whenever he looked at him. His and Daddy's mother was Tess's sister, Jennie, whom Grandad married a year after

Tess's death from breast cancer. Simon was only three and needed a mother, but after a little more than eight years of marriage, Grandad lost Jennie, too.

According to everything I've ever heard about her, my grandma Jennie was a sweet, kind, and loving woman who treated Uncle Simon well, too well for Grandad's liking. It wasn't until after she had died of a heart attack that he moved Simon out of the house and into the barn. According to Uncle Peter, and even Daddy, she wouldn't have tolerated it, even though everyone who knew my grandmother said she was too meek and servile in every other way and permitted Grandad to work her to death. She was often seen beside him in the fields, despite a full day of house cleaning and cooking.

However, Grandad Forman had a religious philosophy that prevented him from ever taking responsibility for anything that had happened to his family or anyone else with whom he might have come into contact. He believed bad things happened to people as a result of their own evil thoughts, evil deeds. God, he preached, punishes us on earth and rewards us on earth. If something terrible happens to someone we all thought was a good person, we must understand that we didn't know what was in his or her heart and in his or her past. God sees all. Grandad was so vehement about this that he often made me feel God was spying on me every moment of the day, and if I should stray so much as an iota from the Good Book or the Commandments, I would be struck down with the speed of a bolt of lightning.

Consequently, Grandad Forman did not cry at funerals, and when the horrible news about Uncle Peter was brought to our house, Grandad absorbed and accepted it, lowered his head, and went out to work in the field just as he had planned.

Mommy was nearly inconsolable. I believe she loved Uncle Peter almost as much as she loved Daddy, almost as much as I loved him. We cried and held each other. Daddy went off to mourn privately, I know. Uncle Simon raged like a wild beast in his barn. We could hear the metal tools being flung against the walls, and then he marched out and took hold of a good size sapling he had planted seven years before and put all of his sorrow into a gigantic effort to lift it, roots and all, out of the earth, which he did.

"Lunatic," Grandad said when he saw what he had done. "God will punish him for that."

That evening I sat on the porch steps and stared up at the stars. I had no appetite at dinner and couldn't pronounce a syllable of grace. I wasn't in the mood to thank God for anything, least of all food, but Grandad thought wasting food was one of the worst sins anyone could commit, so I forced myself to swallow, practically without chewing. Mommy, who cooked and cleaned and kept house for him as well as for

Daddy and me, choked back her tears, but sniffled too often for Grandad's liking. He chastised her: "It's God's will, and His will be done. So stop your confounded sobbing at dinner."

I looked to Daddy to see if he would speak up in her defense, but he stared forward, muted by his sorrow. Unlike Uncle Peter, Daddy was a quiet man, strong and compassionate in his own way, but always, it seemed to me, caught in Grandad's shadow. Grandad Forman was still a powerful man, even in his early seventies. He was about six foot three himself, but walked with stooped shoulders. He reminded me of a closed fist—tight, powerful, even lethal. He had a thick bull neck, was broad-shouldered with long, muscular arms and a small pouch of a stomach. His skin was always dark from working outdoors, and he always had a two- or three-day wire-brush beard because he didn't waste razor blades.

Once, he must have been fairly good-looking. Daddy had inherited his straight nose, dark, brooding eyes, and firm lips, but Daddy was slimmer in build, with well-proportioned shoulders. From the pictures we had of Grandma Jennie, I thought he had inherited her best qualities, too. Despite his quiet manner and his dedication to work, Daddy was nowhere near as hard as Grandad.

"Life's got to go on," Grandad declared, lecturing

to Mommy. "It's God's gift, and we don't turn our backs on it."

Almost for spite, to show us he practiced what he preached, he ate with just as much vigor and appetite as he had ever done, and looked to us to do the same.

I was glad when I could get away from him.

On my tenth birthday, Uncle Peter had bought me a Stradivarius violin. It was very expensive, and Grandad Forman complained for days about the "waste of so much money." But I had taken some lessons at school, and talked about how I had enjoyed playing a violin.

"That's what we need around here," Uncle Peter had decided, "some good music. Honey's just the one to make it for us."

He even paid for my private lessons. My teacher, Clarence Wengrow, claimed I had a natural inclination for it, and early on recommended I think seriously about attending a school of performing arts somewhere. Grandad Forman thought that was pure nonsense, and would actually become angry if we discussed anything about my music at dinner, slapping the table so hard he would make the dishes dance. Uncle Peter tried to get him to appreciate music, but Grandad had a strict puritanical view of it as it being another vehicle upon which the devil rode into our hearts and souls. It took us away from hard work and prayer, and that was always dangerous.

Grandad could go on and on like a hell-and-damnation preacher. Daddy would sit with his head bowed, his eyes closed, like someone just trying to wait out some pain. Most of the time Mommy ignored Grandad, but Uncle Peter always wore a soft smile, as if he found his father quaint, amusing.

I couldn't get Uncle Peter's smile out of my eyes that first night of his death. I heard his laughter and heard him call my name. He loved teasing me about it. Mommy had named me Honey because of my naturally light-brown complexion and the honey color of my hair and my eyes. I understood Grandad Forman immediately let it be known that he didn't think it was proper, but Mommy was able to put up a strong wall of resistence and brush off his tirade of threats and commands.

Uncle Peter would sing, "We've got Honey. We've got sugar, but Honey is the sweet one for me."

He would laugh and throw his arm around my shoulders and kiss the top of my hair, pretending he had just swallowed the most delicious tablespoon of honey in the world.

How could someone with so much life and love in him be snuffed out like a candle in seconds? I wondered. Why would God let this happen? Could Grandad Forman be right? It made no sense to me. I wouldn't accept it. I would never permit myself to think the smallest bad thing about Uncle Peter. He had no secret evil, in his heart or otherwise. It was all simply a galactic mistake, a gross error. God had made a wrong decision or failed to catch it in time. However, I knew if I so much as suggested such a thing in front of Grandad, he would fly into a hurricane of rage.

"Oh, dear God," I prayed, "surely You can right the wrong, correct the error. Turn us back a day and make this day disappear forever," I begged.

Then I picked up my violin and played. My music flowed out into the night. It was an unusually warm spring, so we could enjoy an occasionally tepid evening when the approaching summer let it be known it was nearly at our doorstep.

Suddenly I saw a large shadow move near Uncle Simon's garden, and quickly realized it was he. I stopped playing and went to him. He was sitting on the ground like an Indian at a council meeting, his legs around a flower he had just planted. I could smell the freshly turned earth.

"What's that, Uncle Simon?" I asked.

"For Peter," he said. "He likes these. Snapdragon," he said.

"That's nice, Uncle Simon."

He nodded and pressed the earth around the tiny plant affectionately with his immense fingers, so full of strength and yet so full of gentle kindness and love, too, especially for his precious flowers, his children.

"Play your violin," he said. "Flowers like to hear the music, too."

I knew he often talked to his flowers, which was something that Grandad pointed out as evidence of his being a simpleton. He was the simpleton, not Uncle Simon, as far as I was concerned.

I smiled, knelt beside Uncle Simon, and began to play.

Uncle Peter will always be part of my music, I thought. *I'll always see his smile.*

As long as I played, he lived.

I would play forever.

And we would never say good-bye.

Maybe that was God's way of saying He was sorry, too.

2

—∽∽—

Uncle Simon

We lived in a turn-of-the-century two-story structure with a wraparound porch and nearly fifteen rooms. It was typical of many of the farmhouses in our region of Ohio, houses that were expanded as families grew and their needs increased. The floors were all hardwood. Some rooms had area rugs worn so thin anyone could see the grain of the slats beneath them. Grandad believed in keeping things until they literally fell apart. To replace something merely to change a style or a color was wasteful and therefore sinful. He expected the same sort of sacrifices from his possessions as he did from his family.

All of the art in the house was simple and inexpensive. Most wall mountings consisted of pictures of relatives in dark maple oval frames, all of them captured without smiles on their faces. Daddy explained that, once, people didn't believe in smiling for photographs.

"They thought it wasn't serious and made them look silly if they smiled."

There wasn't one picture of Grandad Forman smiling. Most of the ancestors looked like they suffered from hemorrhoids, I thought, and told Daddy so. He roared with laughter, but warned me never to say such a thing in front of Grandad.

The remainder of our wall hangings consisted of dried flowers pressed under glass, some simple watercolors of country scenes, and lace designs made by Grandad's mother and sisters, all of whom were now gone.

The appliances in the house, including the refrigerator, were nearly twenty years old. Everything had to be repaired as much as possible, even if in the end the repairs would cost more than a replacement. It was true that Grandad was very handy and able to fix most of his machinery himself. He believed the less dependent a man was on anyone, the stronger he was, and the better able he was to live a righteous life. Too many moral compromises were made to satisfy other people, he said.

Mommy wasn't ashamed of what she could do in the house. She kept it very clean and whatever could shine, did shine, but she was too ashamed of the age and the tired look of our furniture to want to invite anyone to our home. I couldn't remember a time when she or Daddy had asked friends to dinner, and we never had a house party.

On occasion my music teacher, Mr. Wengrow, was asked to stay to dinner. He appreciated Mommy's good cooking, but it was easy to see he wasn't fond of sitting across from Grandad, who made negative remarks about his profession. He called it frivolous, and insisted that any activity that wasted our time made us more susceptible to evil. He defined a wasteful activity as anything that didn't provide something useful to touch.

"Music touches our hearts and our minds, our very souls, if you like," Mr. Wengrow suggested softly. I thought that was a beautiful way to put it, but Grandad's reply was simply, "Nonsense and more nonsense."

To Grandad's credit, everything on our farm—the barns, the henhouse, the fields, the equipment—was kept in sparkling clean shape. Dirt, rust, grime, and grease were all treated like symptoms of disease. As soon as I was old enough to bear any responsibility and complete any chore on my own, I was given work. Mommy and I bore all the responsibility for the house itself, but Grandad Forman had me out in the fields bailing hay, helping with the planting and the harvesting, cleaning equipment, picking eggs and feeding chickens as well as cleaning out the henhouses. Often, when the work was really too hard for me, Uncle Simon would instantly be at my side, completing it quickly. I had the feeling he was always watching me, watching over me.

One consequence of having all these chores was the difficulty, if not impossibility of participating in after-school activities along with other students my age. Mommy complained about that, and I think because of her complaints, Grandad restrained his criticism of my violin lessons. At least I had that, thanks to Uncle Peter, who on occasion would stand up to Grandad and argue, which was something Daddy just never would do.

But I never thought Daddy was simply a good son honoring and respecting his father. As I grew older, I became more and more curious about Daddy's relationship with Grandad Forman. I sensed there was something beyond the biblical commandment to honor your parents. There was something else between them, some deep family secret that kept Daddy's eyes from ever turning furious and intent on Grandad, no matter what he said or did to him or to Mommy and me. Rarely did either he or Grandad raise their voices against each other. Grandad's voice was raised in his glaring eyes rather than his clicking tongue, and Daddy choked back any resistance, disapproval, or complaint.

He seemed to go at his work with a fury built out of a need to channel all his unhappiness into something that would please Grandad and, at the same time, give himself some respite, some form of release from the tension that loomed continuously over us all, that darkened our skies, and that kept the shadows on our windows and made us all speak in whispers.

In the evening, when all my chores were done and all my homework, too, I would practice my violin. My room faced the barn, and I could often see Uncle Simon sitting by his open window, listening to me play. He had no television set, nor did he have a radio. For Uncle Simon, watching television in our house was equivalent to my going to a movie in town. Mommy asked him over often, but when he came, if he ever came, he came meekly, moving in tentative steps, waiting for Grandad to bark at him, telling him he should be getting an early night to prepare for the morning's work. Sometimes he did drive him out, but if Mommy protested enough, Grandad backed down and went off muttering to smoke his pipe.

Daddy enjoyed Uncle Simon's company, even if it was only to talk about the farm, the crops, and Uncle Simon's flowers. They also talked about animals and the migrating birds. Daddy knew how close Uncle Simon had been to Uncle Peter. After Uncle Peter's death, Daddy did seem to make more of an effort to spend time with Uncle Simon.

Because Uncle Simon was not usually invited to eat with us, I was to bring him his hot supper.

If Mommy could have her way, Uncle Simon would be invited to eat with us every night, but Grandad complained about how he stank and said it ruined his appetite.

"What do you expect, Pa?" Mommy countered, her Russian accent still quite heavy even after all these years. "He doesn't have a decent place to bathe or shower. That outdoor shower you constructed isn't much, and it's cold water!"

"You don't need to spend hours wasting water. Keeping it cold makes him move faster and waste less," Grandad said.

"You have hot water, don't you?" Mommy fired back at him. Sometimes she showed great courage, and when she did, Grandad always looked for ways to weasel out of the argument, rather than take a fixed position and stubbornly defend it.

"I don't use much of it," he bragged.

"But you have that choice," she continued.

"I won't waste any more time talking nonsense," Grandad proclaimed, and left the room. The upshot was that Uncle Simon was still not welcome on a continual basis, and I was still bringing him his hot food.

I didn't mind doing it, especially after Uncle Peter's death. I, like Daddy, wanted to do what I could to keep the wolf of loneliness away from Uncle Simon's door. The little bit of mirth we had in our lives was gone for him as much as it was for me, I thought.

Most of the time he was waiting for me at the barn door, but occasionally, I brought it up to his makeshift living quarters, furnished with an old, light maplewood table with only two chairs, a bed, and a dresser. Grandad had wired the room so Uncle Simon had a standing lamp and a table lamp. There was a rug Mommy had given him and a pretty worn easy chair, its arms torn in places.

I know it embarrassed him to have me come up the stairs with his food. He'd hurry to stop me at the door, if he could. I offered to sit with him while he ate, but he always told me no. I'd better get back and help my mother or practice my violin.

"Don't know why you send the child over there anyway," Grandad would tell Mommy. "Just leave it on the porch and let him come fetch it. He'll turn her stomach with his pigsty ways."

"Put it out like food for a dog, Grandad? Is that a Christian way to treat so hard a working man?"

Grandad pretended he didn't hear her.

I never paid all that much attention to what Uncle Simon smelled like anyway. All of the odors on the farm seemed to comingle. Mommy practically bathed herself in her cologne before she went shopping with Daddy, and she bathed twice a day, despite Grandad Forman's groaning about wasted water.

"This farm has submersible wells," he lectured. "They could run bone-dry on us one day. Waste not, want not."

"Cleanliness is next to godliness," Mommy fired back at him. Their duels using biblical quotes, quotes from psalms as swords, were sometimes amusing to watch. I knew Mommy enjoyed beating him at his own game. She was always telling him to do unto others as he would have others do unto him. His retort was something like, "That's what I'd expect them to do to me and they're right to do it. Don't forget, an eye for an eye."

To which Mommy would shake her head and say, "And soon we'll all be blind."

Grandad would wave his hand as if he was chasing away gnats and walk off, his head down, his long arms swinging in rhythm to his plodding gait.

When did he ever laugh? When did he ever feel happy or good about himself? Why was he so worried about sinning and going to hell?

Maybe he thought he was already in hell. It wasn't to be very long before I would understand why.

3

---❦---

Tears on My Pillow

Uncle Peter's death remained vivid and depressing, a burden I could not easily unload. Sometimes, I would just stop doing my homework and start crying. Sometimes, I woke up in the middle of the night and pressed my face to my pillow to stifle the tears. My throat ached from holding down my grief. No matter how clear the day, how blue the sky, it looked gray and overcast to me. I spent my free time walking alone, my hands in the pockets of my jeans, my head down. It was even difficult to play the violin, because when I did, it made me think of him and I made mistakes. Mr. Wengrow abruptly ended my first lesson after Uncle Peter's death and told me I was just not ready to return to my daily life. He was sympathetic and told me grief, especially grief over someone very dear to you, becomes a part of who and what you are and is not easily put aside.

"Give yourself a little more time," he advised.

I didn't want him to leave. I was caught between my great sorrow and great guilt, feeling I was letting down Uncle Peter and his memory. Both Daddy and Mommy were very concerned. They both knew that, except for when I had to eat with Grandad, I barely touched my food. Even the simplest of my farm chores became nearly impossible. Uncle Simon was everywhere, covering for me so that Grandad Forman wouldn't complain. Many times I found my work had already been done before I arrived to do it. I knew it wasn't fair. Uncle Simon had more to do than most people, even for someone as big and powerful as he was.

The few friends I had at school began to avoid me. I knew why. I knew I was too depressing to them, and there was just so much time they wanted to give my period of mourning. They wanted to talk about their flirtations, their music and television programs, and here I was staring at the lunch table in dark silence, not listening to what they were saying and not caring.

I didn't watch television or listen to music and had no interest in going to the movies or on trips with anyone who asked, so they stopped asking. I felt like a balloon that had broken loose and was drifting in the wind aimlessly, carried in whatever direction the breeze was going, and slowly sinking into darkness.

Finally, one night when I had wandered off after dinner, Daddy came out to find me. I had gone down to the pond and sat on the small dock, my feet dangling only an inch or so from the inky water. Around me, the peepers were conducting a choral symphony, punctuated occasionally with a splash when a bullfrog leapt into the water. Because of the way the stars danced on the water and the solitude here, the pond was one of Uncle Peter's and my favorite places.

"Hey," I heard Daddy say, and turned in surprise to see him walking toward me. "Why aren't you doing homework or practicing your violin?" he asked when he was beside me.

"I have it all done, Daddy. I did it in study session today."

"Okay, but I've gotten used to hearing that violin," he said.

I looked out at the dark water.

"Uncle Peter would be pretty upset, after all he did to get you started," Daddy said softly. "I told you I was going to continue paying for your lessons."

"I know." I choked back my tears.

Daddy then did something he had never done before. He sat next to me on the dock, keeping his feet just above the water, too. For a long moment neither of us spoke. The silence seemed to engulf us like a warm blanket. I imagined his arm around my shoulders, just the way Uncle Peter would embrace me occasionally and laugh or try to cheer me up.

"I miss him a great deal, too," Daddy said. "Every time I hear someone laugh, I turn to see if Peter is coming through a door or over the field toward me. I warned him about doing that crop dusting, but he was so carefree about everything in his life. He just refused to see danger or evil anywhere. He was too pure a spirit."

"I know," I said. A fugitive tear started to run down my left cheek. I flicked it off quickly, the way I might flick off a fly.

"However, the last thing Peter would want is for all of us to stop living, too, Honey. You know that, right?"

I nodded.

"It just hurts too much, Daddy. I can't be anything like Grandad and I don't want to be," I said defiantly.

He was silent and then he nodded.

"No, I don't want you to be like him, either," he admitted.

"I don't think he really loves any of us," I continued.

"I guess he does in his own way, Honey."

I shook my head.

"You don't accept terrible things happening to people you love as easily as he does."

"You don't know how he mourns or when. He does, in his own way," Daddy insisted. "It doesn't do any good to dislike him. It doesn't bring Peter back. Did you ever hear Peter speak against him?"

"Not in so many words," I admitted. "But he didn't approve of him," I insisted.

"I think he felt sorry for him. That's the last thing Grandad wants, however," Daddy warned, "anyone feeling sorry for him."

Why not? I wondered. What was so terrible about people showing you sympathy?

We were both quiet again. Then Daddy reached out and put his arm around my shoulders.

"I don't want to see you so unhappy so long, and your mother is very worried about you, Honey," he said.

"Did she send you out?"

"No, I'm here because I'm just as worried," he told me.

I relaxed and let my head fall against his shoulder.

"What all this does, Daddy, is make me afraid of ever loving anyone else. It's like what happened when we lost Kasey Lady."

I was referring to our beautiful golden retriever, who had eaten some rat poison Grandad set out for rodents in the henhouse.

"Mm," Daddy said. He loved that dog, too.

"After we buried her, Mommy told you she never

wanted to have another animal. She couldn't take the pain of loss."

"She'll change her mind one of these days, or the first time she sets eyes on another cute puppy.

"People lose people all the time, Honey. You can't stop it and you can't stop yourself from loving someone. It isn't like turning the lights on and off. It has its own life, its own power, and sweeps over you."

"Is that what happened to you, Daddy? Is that why you and Mommy got married?" I asked.

He was quiet and then he laughed.

"No," he said. "Hardly."

"What do you mean?"

"Our situation was somewhat reversed. We got married first and then fell in love," he revealed.

I pulled back and looked up at him.

"I don't understand. How do you do that?"

"Well, after your grandmother Jennie had died, Grandad Forman decided we needed a woman on the farm. He wasn't going to remarry. He said he was too old and God didn't mean for him to have a wife, but I wasn't exactly burning up the world with my romantic skills. Matter of fact, I hadn't had a girlfriend since the tenth grade, and she got married to someone else a day after graduation.

"Oh, I had a date here and there, or what you would roughly call a date, I guess, meeting someone at a dance or at the movies, but nothing ever became anything. Peter was seeing lots of women, but he was too free a soul to give any woman the sense she'd be important enough to be his wife forever and ever. He liked what he called 'playing the field.'

"There were many nights when he and Grandad went at it, Grandad ridiculing and criticizing Peter's lifestyle, even calling him sinful and warning him that God would not look kindly on him."

"I'm sure he believes Uncle Peter's death was because of that, doesn't he?" I asked quickly.

Daddy looked away.

"Maybe."

After a moment, he turned back to me.

"Anyway, it was clear that the obligation to bring a woman into our lives fell on my shoulders."

He paused and tossed a pebble into the lake.

"You know your mother came here when she was only just nineteen."

"With her aunt, yes," I said.

"Well, Grandad was impatient with my failure to just go out and find a wife, so he contacted Mommy's aunt Ethel, who brought your mother to America to marry me."

"What are you saying, Daddy? You mean, she knew she was coming here to marry you, even though she had never seen you before?"

He nodded.

"And Grandad arranged it?"

"Yes."

"But why would Mommy do that?"

"Things were hard for her where she lived in Russia, and this was an opportunity to escape it."

He laughed.

"I'll never forget the way we were introduced. Your grandad said, 'Here's your wife. The wedding will be tomorrow.' "

"But why did you do it? I mean, I know Mommy is very pretty and all, but she was still a stranger. How can you marry someone without knowing anything about her?"

"When I first saw your mother that day, I actually felt sorrier for her than I had been feeling for myself. No one looked more helpless, more lost, more terrified of tomorrow. I couldn't even utter the word no.

"And then I looked into her eyes, past the fear, past the terror, and I saw something that warmed my heart. I don't know if that qualifies as love at first sight, but I thought I could make her feel good, and I hoped she could do the same for me.

"In time, we grew closer and closer. Maybe we didn't have the sort of romantic start people see in movies and read in books, but what we have is strong. We've become tied to each other in deep ways. I don't think she could stop herself from loving me any more than I could stop myself from loving her.

"If that could happen to me, it will surely happen to you, Honey. Don't worry about it. Love will find its way into your heart, and it will be more comfortable there because of what your uncle Peter gave you and taught you."

"I hope so, Daddy."

"I know so," he said. He smiled at me and stood up. "How about you come home and practice that violin?"

"Okay, Daddy," I said, and rose. He reached for my hand.

"Look at you," he said, "with calluses on your palms from your farm chores. I bet that alone scares away most of the boys today. You're too tough for them."

I laughed.

"I haven't held hands with any lately," I said.

"Never mind, you will," he said.

I couldn't remember the two of us having a more warm and wonderful conversation. It did help me regain my composure, and that night, I played the violin better than I had for weeks. When I looked out the window, I saw Uncle Simon had come to his. I couldn't see the expression on his face, only his big body was silhouetted in the frame, but I knew that he was wearing a smile. I could feel it even across the yard.

* * *

I never stopped mourning the death of Uncle Peter, but in the days that followed my quiet conversation with Daddy at the pond, I felt myself emerging from the darkness and looking forward to the light. I began to talk more at school, cared more about my appearance, and practiced my violin with greater determination. Mr. Wengrow was very pleased with my progress and told me so.

One day he made a surprising proposal.

"I have another student I tutor. He's a pianist, and I think it might be of great benefit to you both if you practiced some music together. I don't know if it's possible, but I would suggest you come to my home to do so. I have a piano there. What do you think of the idea?

"Actually," he said before I could respond, "the two of you are my most exciting and promising students. I would want to give you both extra help and not charge you for it. I wouldn't be in this work if I didn't have a passion for it and I didn't get great satisfaction out of finding students like yourself and Chandler," he added.

"Chandler? You don't mean Chandler Maxwell?" I asked.

Chandler Maxwell was a very wealthy boy in my class whom everyone considered to be the poster boy for being stuck-up. Except for some geeky younger boys who seemed to idolize him, he had no friends whatsoever. He came to school in a shirt and tie, with his hair trimmed almost military style and his slacks perfectly creased. There wasn't a single school activity that appeared to interest him. He didn't belong to any team, any group, any club. Everyone had the feeling he was looking down on their efforts, and everyone wondered why he didn't attend some expensive private school anyway.

Apparently, his father, who was president of one of the local banks, didn't believe in sending him to a private school. He had succeeded with a public school education and his son should do the same was the philosophy he preached to anyone who asked.

Most of us knew Chandler played piano. There were times when he played it at school, and the choral teacher and the band instructor both tried to get him to participate in their concerts, but he steadfastly refused, simply shaking his head with a smirk that suggested he thought their suggestion was ridiculous.

Naturally, the other boys mocked him, teased him, even tried to get him to fight, but he never did. If I could say anything on his behalf it was that he had remarkable self-control and the ability to ignore anyone and anything that displeased him.

He was not bad-looking, either. There were occasions when I stared at him and his eyes met mine, but he always made me feel guilty, made me feel as if I had stolen a look at a forbidden subject. I know I turned crimson and shifted my eyes away guiltily, and then chastised myself for being so interested, even for an instant. I wanted to hate him and despise him as much as all my friends did, but something kept me from doing that, something kept me stealing glances.

"Yes," Mr. Wengrow said. "Chandler Maxwell. I've already discussed the possibility with him and he is willing, especially after I described your talent."

"Maybe he won't think I'm so talented once he hears me play," I said.

"Chandler respects my opinion on such matters, Honey. He wouldn't be working with me otherwise, believe me. He's a very opinionated and an extraordinarily self-confident young man. Personally, I think he has musical genius."

I raised my eyebrows. I knew Chandler was a good student, but not within the top ten students in my class. He was in all of my classes—including my language class, even though I suspected he didn't have any interest in taking Spanish. He always looked so bored, but took it because there was a language requirement. Whenever he was asked to pronounce or recite something, he did it so softly Mrs. Howard had to ask him to repeat it, and eventually would give up on him.

"I don't know," I said.

The idea was intriguing, but at the same time

frightening. What if he made fun of me? I knew how sarcastic he could be. Most of the boys who jeered him didn't even understand his comebacks and how degrading and nasty they were. When that happened, I could see the self-satisfaction in his eyes. If he caught me looking at him, he tightened his lips and narrowed his eyes with suspicion, as if he was afraid I might expose him.

"Well, would you like me to speak to your mother about it?" Mr. Wengrow asked. "Because of her background, she has a real appreciation for good music."

"I don't know," I repeated.

"Well, let me mention it and then you and your family can discuss it. I suppose there would be some consideration about getting you to my home and back."

"I have my license," I said quickly. "I've been driving since I was ten, actually. On the farm, I mean. I'm sure I could use my daddy's pickup."

I realized I was solving problems enthusiastically. I did want to do this.

"Fine. We'll talk about it in more detail next time I come," he said.

Before he left, he did talk to Mommy and Daddy. Grandad was present, but made no comments, unless we counted his grunt.

"It sounds like a good opportunity," Mommy told

me later that night. "Mr. Wengrow's so excited about it, he says he won't charge for the added time. What do you think, Honey?"

"I guess I could try to see how it goes," I offered.

Daddy looked pleased and nodded.

They were both so nervous about my moods and emotions these days that anything that promised to bring me some pleasure was desirable.

"Then we'll tell him it's fine with us," Mommy said.

"I'll need the pickup, I think," I told Daddy. "I wouldn't want you to have to drive me."

"You can use the pickup, but you had better clean it up before you get in it," Mommy said. "You don't want to walk into someone's home smelling like a farm girl."

"What's wrong with that?" we heard Grandad call from the living room. He was listening through the walls.

"Nothing a good shampoo and bath won't cure," Mommy retorted.

Daddy actually laughed loud enough for Grandad to hear.

It brought a smile to my face.

Uncle Peter wouldn't have laughed much louder, I thought. He's still with us.

4

The Lesson

Needless to say, I was very nervous the first night I drove over to Mr. Wengrow's house. I rushed through dinner, which brought me looks of displeasure from Grandad Forman's piercing, reprimanding eyes, and then I went upstairs to my room and agonized over what I should wear.

Should it be one of my better dresses or skirts, or should I just wear what I wore to school? Was I making too much of all this? Would I be overdoing it, pumping up Chandler's already exaggerated ego? What if I dressed nicely but he pulled a complete switch and came in a pair of jeans and a T-shirt, showing me how little he thought of the occasion? Wouldn't I feel the fool?

And then what about my hair? Should I have washed it? Was brushing it and spraying it enough? How much makeup should I put on? Just lipstick, or a little rouge? I kept smelling myself, terrified that I would bring the farm odors along with me. Chandler would surely say something unpleasant about that. I was positive I overdid my cologne.

Finally, I settled on just a little touch of lipstick, no rouge, and my dark blue skirt and light blue short-sleeve blouse. I put on a pair of sandals, took one last glimpse of myself in the mirror, and hurried downstairs, not realizing until I was at the bottom that I had forgotten my violin.

Mumbling complaints about myself to myself, I hurried back upstairs to fetch it and then took a deep breath, calmed myself, and walked slowly down the stairs. Mommy came out to tell me to drive carefully.

"Come right home afterward, Honey," Daddy called from behind her.

When I stepped out of the house, I saw that Uncle Simon had washed the truck. He was just wiping off the windshield, and stepped away as I approached.

"I told your daddy I would do it," he said before I could ask or say a word.

"Thank you, Uncle Simon."

"I checked the air in the tires and the oil, too," he added. "Everything's fine."

"I'm only going about four miles, Uncle Simon," I said, smiling. "It's not more than a ten-minute ride," I added.

"Most accidents happen close to home," he said. I realized everyone was nervous about everyone else since Uncle Peter's accident.

"I'll be careful," I promised, opening the truck door, putting in my violin, and turning back to him. He stood there, nodding.

"Thank you, Uncle Simon," I said again, and got on tiptoe to give him a quick kiss on his cheek. Even in the darkness, I could see his face bloom like one of his red roses. His eyes brightened.

I got into the truck, waved, and drove off, taking a hard bounce on the rise in the driveway Grandad never cared to have fixed because it reminded us that "life was full of bumps to avoid or tolerate."

Moments later, I was on the highway. My heart sped up with my anticipated arrival at Mr. Wengrow's. When I pulled into his driveway, I realized I would have to park next to Chandler's beautiful late-model black Mercedes. I pulled as far from it as I could.

Mr. Wengrow lived in a modest one-story Queen Anne, set back on close to an acre of land. He was a bachelor who had lived with his parents. His mother had passed away first and his father had died just last year. During the day he taught music at a private elementary school.

Mr. Wengrow greeted me in a dark brown sports jacket, an open shirt, and a pair of brown slacks and shoes. I was glad to see he wasn't dressed any more formally than usual.

There was a very small vestibule on entry with a mirror on the right. The frame of the mirror had hooks for jackets and beneath it was a small, dark oak table with a flower-patterned vase. It had nothing in it, and I regretted not asking Uncle Simon for some flowers to bring.

"Right on time," he said smiling. "Chandler was a little early. He likes to spend more time warming up," he explained, raising his voice over the sound of the piano, which seemed to get louder.

He led me to the living room on the left. It had modest, colonial furnishings with a large dark brown oval rug. The grand piano was prominent, actually too large for the room, which was well-lit by a ceiling fixture and two standing lamps, as well as the small lamp on the piano. Mr. Wengrow had set up my music stand to the right, with its clipped light already on and waiting for my sheet music.

Chandler was dressed like he dressed for school, a tie and slacks. He didn't look up or stop playing when I entered. Both Mr. Wengrow and I watched him for a few moments and then Mr. Wengrow nodded toward my stand. I took my violin out of its case and stepped up. Chandler finally lifted his fingers from the keys and turned to me.

"I didn't know you were taking private lessons," he said.

I wanted to say, *How would you know? You never say two words to me at school,* but instead, I nodded and said, "Mr. Wengrow just told me about you, too."

"Oh?" He looked at our teacher.

"Don't you two see each other at school?" he asked innocently. "I just assumed..."

I looked at Chandler.

"We see each other," he said, his eyes softening and becoming impish, I thought. "But we've never exchanged résumés," he added.

"Well, now you both know. Shall we begin?" Mr. Wengrow said, and started to outline what he hoped to accomplish.

Almost immediately I made one mistake after another, and sounded like a first-year student. I became even more flustered because of that and made more mistakes.

"Take your time," Mr. Wengrow kept saying.

Every time we had to stop, Chandler lifted his fingers off the keys but held them hovering there and stared ahead. He said nothing encouraging. Finally, he stood up.

"Why don't you work with her for a few minutes solo, Mr. Wengrow? I have to make a phone call anyway," he added and, without waiting for a response, walked out of the room.

I felt like bursting into tears.

"I'm sorry," I said.

"It's all right. Every time you do something different, you'll have some butterflies. With time and experience, you'll find ways to overcome it, I'm sure. Let's go back and do this one more time," he urged patiently.

After a while I did feel myself calm down. When Chandler returned, he glanced at me quickly but took his place at the piano and waited for Mr. Wengrow's instructions. We played on and I did better and better, so much better, in fact, that Chandler started to glance at me, his eyes revealing appreciation.

"Good," Mr. Wengrow muttered, nodding. "Good. That's it. Good. Well, Chandler," he said stepping back when we ended, "was I right about Miss Lester or not?"

"You were very much right," Chandler said, glancing at me and then standing.

"Shall we say same time, same night next week?" Mr. Wengrow asked.

"It's fine with my schedule," Chandler said.

"Honey?"

"What? Oh, yes," I said.

"Good night, Mr. Wengrow," Chandler said, and started out. I put my violin away quickly.

"You both have the makings of fine musicians, Honey," Mr. Wengrow said. "I have high hopes."

"Thank you," I said. I heard the front door open and close.

He has as much personality as a dead snail, I thought. I felt stupid now even worrying about what I wore, what I looked like. I almost wished I had smelled like a cow when I arrived. *He needs something sharp stinging his nostrils,* I concluded. I never knew a boy could stir such rage in me without saying a word.

Mr. Wengrow followed me to the door to say good night. I thanked him and left, my head down as I walked.

"Watch your step," I heard, and looked up quickly to see Chandler waiting at his car, leaning against it, his arms folded.

"You drove that truck?" he asked, nodding at it.

"It didn't drive me," I replied.

He smiled and nodded.

"I know your farm. My father's bank carries the mortgage."

I knew his father was a bank president, of course, but I had no idea where Grandad Forman had his business affairs. I didn't reply. I went to the truck, opened the door, and put the violin on the seat.

"You are good," he said, stepping closer to me. "I trusted Mr. Wengrow not to waste my time, but he sometimes exaggerates to make the parents of his students feel good about their so-called prodigies."

"My parents don't think I'm a prodigy. Is that what yours think you are?" I shot back at him. "Is that why you play the piano?"

He shrugged.

"I don't know. Maybe. I play because it pleases me and seems to please people who hear me do it. Why do you play the violin?" he countered.

I thought a moment.

"An uncle of mine once said I don't play it."

"Huh?"

"He said, 'It plays you.' "

"It plays you?"

"Exactly," I said, getting into the truck and looking out the window at him. "If you can find a way to understand that, you might find a way to understand yourself."

"Who says I don't understand myself?"

"No one. Who else can know if you do or not but you?"

I started the engine. He drew closer.

"What are you, full of riddles?"

"Not any more or less than anyone else, I suppose. I enjoyed playing my violin with your accompaniment, Chandler. You don't play the piano. It plays you," I said, smiling, and put the truck in reverse.

I backed out of the driveway and took one last

look at him. He was still standing there, watching me. I waved and then drove off, my heart thumping so hard, I thought I would have a rush of blood to my head and pass out.

He has beautiful eyes, I admitted to myself. He didn't turn them to me as much as I would have liked, but on the other hand, if he looked at me too much, I would probably have a harder time concentrating on my music. Still, it was nice to think of them now. It brought a smile to my face, and that smile remained there like a soft impression in newly fallen snow.

"You look like you had a good time," Daddy said when I entered the house. He and Mommy were in the kitchen, talking. Grandad had fallen asleep in his chair in front of the television set. He was snoring at a volume that was almost as loud as the program.

"What? Oh. Yes, it was very good, Daddy."

"I'm glad," he said. "Maybe you really should think of a career in music."

"Maybe," I said, and went up to my room.

I sat at my vanity table and stared at my image in the mirror, wondering if I was at all attractive. Was my nose too small, my lips too thin, my eyes too close together?

I stood up and began to undress, gazing at myself as I stripped down to bare skin. I had a figure people called perky, cute. Would I ever be beautiful? It seemed to me that boys didn't take cute girls seriously enough, only the girls who were beautiful. I'd always look too young. When I once voiced such a complaint, Mommy told me to just wait twenty years, I'd love being considered too young then; but who wanted to wait so long to be happy about herself? Not me. I wanted to be happy about myself now.

I realized I was standing nude in front of my mirror and judging my breasts, my curves, and my waist. Was this sinful? Would I be punished for my vanity? Grandad would certainly say so, I thought, and I almost expected to hear a boom of thunder and see the sizzle of God's displeasure light up my bedroom windows.

I heard the phone ring and a moment later Mommy called up to me.

"There's a phone call for you, Honey."

"Me?" I scooped up my robe and hurriedly put it on as I went to the foot of the stairs. Mommy was standing at the bottom. "Who is it?"

"Chandler Maxwell. He sounds so formal." Mommy shook her head and laughed. "He sounds more like one of your teachers than a classmate."

"Yes, he does," I said, laughing to myself. *What could he want?* I wondered. *Did he get angry at me for teasing him? Is he calling to tell me he won't attend another lesson?*

We had one phone, situated in the hallway. Grandad didn't see any need for another and certainly didn't see a need for me to have my own phone, so there wasn't that much privacy for anyone who received a call—not that I received very many.

"Hello," I said. Mommy walked back into the kitchen.

"I'm sorry to bother you so late."

"It's not that late."

"Yes, well, for many people it might be," he insisted.

"Well, what is it?"

"I have tickets to the production of *Porgy and Bess* at the convention center. It's light opera."

"I know what it is," I said.

"It probably won't be that good, but my father gets these tickets because of the bank, and I was wondering if you would like to go. It's this coming Saturday night. I know that's giving you very short notice," he added before I could respond, "so I won't be upset if you can't go. I just thought you might enjoy the music. We have so little of it in our community and—"

"Yes," I said to stop him from going on and on.

"Yes?"

"Yes, I'd like to go. Thank you."

"Oh, well, good. I'll see you in school and give you more detail."

"That's fine. Thank you."

"Maybe..."

He hesitated. I waited a moment and then said, "Yes?"

"Maybe, if you're able to, you could, I mean, I could take you for something to eat first."

"Oh. Sure. I guess," I said.

"Fine. I'll give you more detail in school," he repeated.

"Okay."

"Well, then, good night. See you very soon, I hope," he said.

"I'll see you in school tomorrow, Chandler," I reminded him, laughing to myself. I didn't think anyone could be more nervous and shy than I was. I now suspected that most of what people interpreted as his arrogance was just his shyness.

"Right. See you then," he said and hung up.

"What was that all about?" Mommy asked from the kitchen doorway.

"Chandler Maxwell's father gets tickets to shows and he wanted to know if I'd like to go see *Porgy and Bess* Saturday night. I said yes. Is that all right?"

"That's very nice," Mommy said. Daddy came up beside her.

"He wants to take me to dinner first," I added.

"Well, that's a full-blown date. Sounds like something special," Daddy kidded.

"She could use something new to wear," Mommy told him. He nodded.

"I don't have to buy something new," I said.

"Your mother wants you to so she can help you pick it out," Daddy said, smiling at her.

"But…"

"He's right," Mommy said, stepping forward to take my hand and smile. "There's a point in every mother's life when she starts to relive her own youth through her children, especially a daughter."

I smiled. It wasn't something she and I had done very often.

"Okay," I said. Then I ran up the stairs, my heavy footsteps waking Grandad, who called out to ask what was going on in his house? It sounded like the roof was caving in. Couldn't we walk softer?

Not tonight, I thought. Not tonight, Grandad. I was so excited, I didn't think I would fall asleep. I got into my nightgown and under the covers, anxious for the night to pass and the morning to bring me to school.

I reached over and turned off the light on my nightstand, throwing the room into darkness.

Outside, the moon had just gone over the west side of the house. Like a giant yellow spotlight, it lit up the barn and my step-uncle Simon's window. He was sitting there, looking toward mine.

And I realized I had left it wide open while I had been studying my naked body. Had he been there that whole time? I was too old now to leave my window open like this, I thought, and went over to draw the shade.

After all, I told myself, *Chandler Maxwell had called me for a date.* I would buy something new and beautiful and I would fix my hair and study how beautiful women in magazines did their makeup. Men would start to notice me. It would be as if I had just been discovered standing there or walking or sitting at a table.

Who is that? they would surely wonder. Every smile, every look of appreciation would be like hands clapping.

Emerging from childhood, a woman is surely reborn. It's almost as if a light goes on inside us and the glow from it brightens the stage and opens the curtain. When that happens, one way or another, all of us live off the applause.

5

⸺❦⸺

A New Song Begins

I used to think that I was exceptionally shy. If a boy stopped to speak to me or showed me any attention, I could feel the heat rise to my face immediately, and just knowing my skin was starting to glow like the inside of a toaster made me even shier. I had to shift my eyes away and always spoke quickly, giving whomever it was the impression I wanted to get away from him as fast as I could. It wasn't my intention, but I could understand why someone would think that.

When I arrived at school the following day, I looked forward to seeing Chandler. His locker was halfway down the hall from mine, and pretty soon I saw him arrive. He glanced my way, but to my surprise, he returned his attention to his locker, took out what he needed, closed it, and walked on as if he and I had never met. For a moment I was so stunned I had to question my own sanity. Did we speak on the phone and did he invite me to dinner and a show? Or was that a dream?

I hurried to homeroom, now even more curious and more eager to speak with him. He sat two rows left of me. When I entered, I looked at him, but he had his face in one of his textbooks as usual, not bothering to look up when the teacher spoke or when the announcements came over the public-address system. Our teacher asked everyone to take his or her seat. Roll was taken and then the bell for our first class rang. I deliberately moved slowly so Chandler and I would be side by side as we were leaving the room.

"Hi," I said as soon as he was beside me.

"Hi," he replied; he gazed about nervously for a moment and then sped up and walked away, swinging the briefcase he carried, which looked like a lawyer's attaché case and was the object of many jokes.

I just stood there, amazed, as other students moved by, some knocking into me because my feet were planted in cement.

"You all right?" Karen Jacobs asked me.

"What? Oh. Yes," I said and started to walk to class. She tagged along.

Karen was a mousy-looking girl with big though

dull brown eyes, whose life was apparently so boring she fed off everyone else's sadness as well as happiness. Almost ninety percent of what she said to anyone daily was in the form of a question. Sometimes I thought she resembled a squirrel, hoarding information, tidbits, anecdotes about other people, like acorns; information, tidbits, anecdotes about other people, and sometimes, I thought she was more like a parasite, existing solely off the life of her hosts, which in this case was anyone who cared to share his or her revelations.

"I saw you say something to Chandler Maxwell. What did you say?"

"I said hi."

"Why?"

"Why not?" I fired back at her. She looked confused and lagged a step or two behind me.

During my first-period class, however, I sensed her nearly constant study of my every glance and gesture. Maybe she had some sort of built-in radar for these sort of things. Whatever she had, she honed in on my interest in Chandler and made us the subject of her study for the day. I knew she was eager for gossip she could use to ingratiate herself with some of the other students, especially the girls in our class who made no effort to hide their dislike of her.

As it turned out, this was exactly what Chandler was trying to avoid. Between periods one and two, as we were moving through the corridor, he swooped up beside me and said, "Here."

He had a slip of paper in his hand. For a moment I didn't know what he wanted. He repeated, "Here," and I took the paper. The moment I did, he walked away. When I paused to open the note, Karen moved closer. I felt her approaching and I shoved the paper into my math text.

"Didn't Chandler Maxwell just hand you something?" she asked me.

I turned to her.

"Yes."

"What was it, something secret between you?"

I was annoyed, but for some reason, I decided to lie.

"I dropped some notes when I left English literature just now, and he picked them up and gave them to me. Why didn't you say something about it?"

"I didn't see you drop anything," she insisted.

"How could you miss it?" I countered. "You've been watching me like a hawk."

"I have not," she protested, but fell back as if I had just slapped her face.

I knew she was just waiting for me to take out the note in my next class, so I deliberately pretended no interest. I don't know why it was so important to me to be surreptitious, but it was obviously important to Chandler, so I maintained the same very low profile.

It wasn't until I had time to go to the girls' room

that I took out the note and read it. It was, as he promised, details about Saturday night: what time he would pick me up, where he would take me for dinner, what time the show started and ended, and what time I could expect to be home. He hadn't even signed it or anything. I was disappointed, but I was more angry. How could he be so impersonal and so insensitive? Was I the first girl he had ever taken on a date? Maybe he didn't know how to behave.

That did give me reason to pause. Maybe I was his first real date, too. Why did I assume that he had taken other girls out? No one ever spoke about it. If anyone would know, it would certainly be Karen Jacobs, and I never heard her pass any gossip along concerning him.

I was hoping he would be friendlier at lunch. Chandler usually sat with some computer heads in the rear of the cafeteria. I was ahead of him in the line and deliberately found an empty table, anticipating his joining me; but he didn't. He went to his usual place and, moments later, some of the girls in my class, including Karen, sat at my table. I could see from the looks on their faces that Karen had begun to spread a story. I decided she was going to be the editor of the *National Enquirer* one day.

"Is something going on between you and Chandler Maxwell?" Susie Weaver asked me almost immediately. She was a very attractive red-haired girl who was

already dating college boys and had an air of sophistication about her that made her the target of every other
girl's envy. All of us, including me, hung on her every
comment and pronouncement as if it were relationship
gospel. Her seal of approval on a boy someone was
seeing was sought after and appreciated, and when she
condemned someone, everyone joined the bandwagon
and found faults where none really existed.

"Why?" I replied, which was a mistake. I should
have either vehemently denied it, if I wanted to deny
it, or owned up to it and defended it.

Her lips softened and spread like two strips of but-
ter on a frying pan.

"How long have you been sneaking around with
him?" she followed.

The other girls smiled, and Karen looked so self-
satisfied, I felt like smearing my piece of pizza over
her pudgy blah face.

"I haven't been sneaking around with him or anyone else," I said.

"Really?" Susie looked at the others. She wore a
look of achievement, the expression of some investi-
gator who had just exposed the criminal. The others
nodded. "You don't have to be ashamed. Unless you
and Chandler are doing something pretty kinky,"
Susie added, and started eating.

"I'm not ashamed. There's nothing like that
going on!"

"Or embarrassed."

"I'm not!" I practically screamed.

"Do you go to his place, or do you take him into your barn with the cows?"

"Stop it!"

"Sensitive, isn't she?" Susie asked the others. All eyes were on me.

I took a deep breath, calming myself.

"Chandler and I are taking private music lessons together, if you have to know," I finally confessed. "We have the same teacher, and he's having us practice duets, me on the violin and Chandler on the piano."

"So, you admit you're making music together," Susie said, and the whole table roared and giggled with laughter. "I hope you're on key and in rhythm."

Their laughter was louder.

"Does he say please first and thank you afterward?" Janice Handley asked. She was Susie's alter ego, her gofer, ready to jump at her beck and call.

There was more laughter.

My face turned white before it turned scarlet. I glanced back at Chandler. He was looking my way now, an expression of concern and disgust on his face.

"Come on," Susie said in a mock-friendly tone of voice, "tell us about it. You can trust us. We're all your friends."

"Some friends," I said. I glared at Karen. "Are you satisfied? Think they like you any more than they did before school started today?"

I rose, picked up my tray, and left the table, their laughter roaring like a waterfall behind me. I sat out the remainder of my lunch hour in a stall in the girls' room. Two of the girls who had been at the table came in, and I heard them talking and laughing about me and Chandler. What interested me was their conclusion that he and I were made for each other. Somehow, because I was unable to participate in after-school activities and did so little with them and the others, they interpreted it to mean I was just as snobby.

As I was entering Spanish class, Chandler caught up with me.

"Don't take the school bus home," he said. "I'll take you. Just wait at your locker."

He spoke quickly, like someone giving very secret information about an impending rebellion, and then took his seat and ignored me the rest of the period. Every once in a while, I saw some of my classmates looking my way, whispering and then laughing to themselves.

It was as if my eyes were washed with a good dose of reality and opened wider. Susie Weaver wasn't as sophisticated as I had thought. None of them were. Maybe they were out there, doing things I never did:

drinking, smoking, hanging out late into the night, being sexually active, but that didn't make them sophisticated. They suddenly all looked like immature people dressed in adult clothes. Most of them were just as insecure as I was, if not more so, and what they did was mock me or someone else in order to cover up the truth about themselves.

I used to feel terrible about not having loads of friends, not being invited to parties, not dating regularly, not being Miss Popularity, and being thought of as a prude, too religious, too moral, but now I felt relieved, even lucky. What I felt terrible about missing looked more than simply insignificant. It looked foolish, wasteful. Maybe there was too much Grandad in me, but I wasn't feeling sorry about it.

I guess I really was an outsider, a loner of sorts. I guess Chandler and I did appear made for each other. I hurried to my locker after class and waited eagerly for him. He deliberately lingered until most of the school had left. When that bell ending the day rang, it was often like a stampede. Anyone watching outside would think we had all just been released from doing hard time in a state penitentiary.

"What happened in the lunch room?" he asked me as soon as he approached.

I told him how Karen Jacobs had seen him pass me the note and then had made a big thing of it with the others who enjoyed teasing me.

"What did they say?"

"Stupid stuff," I replied. "I wouldn't honor it by repeating a word."

He nodded.

"That was why I didn't bother you all day. I was afraid of something like that. I know I'm the source of amusement for many of these yahoos."

I laughed at his reference to *Gulliver's Travels*, which we had been studying in English—yahoos were human creatures who were dirtier and more stupid than talking horses.

"I just thought what you and I did wasn't any of their business," he continued. "I thought—no, correction, I *knew* they would pick on you if you had anything to do with me."

"You didn't have to worry about me," I said, my eyes narrowing with angry determination. "They don't bother me. I can take care of myself."

He nodded.

"I wasn't worrying about that. I was worrying that you would..."

"What?"

"Get driven away and change your mind," he admitted. He looked back so he could avoid my eyes.

"I'm not that easily influenced, Chandler. I'm not going to go out with someone or not go out with someone because of what *they* think. I have a mind of my own," I insisted. "You should have known that."

He looked at me and nodded.

"I do now," he said, and then we both laughed. It felt good. It felt as if I had been holding in some happiness the whole day and it was ready to explode.

"I'll take you home," he said, and we left the building.

He kept his car so well, it looked new. The leather smelled wonderful and felt soft to the touch. He had a built-in CD player and a telephone, too. I was very impressed, but I didn't want to seem like someone who had never been off the farm.

"It happened to me once before," he said after a few minutes of driving.

"What?"

"Something like this. I was in the tenth grade. You probably don't remember, but I was going with Audra Lothrop for a week or so. Her friends really made fun of her and turned her against me. I decided most of the girls in this school are lollipops."

"Lollipops?"

"Shiny, sweet, and insubstantial," he recited. "You're the first girl I've spent any time with who is focused on something other than her hairdo."

"That's not true, Chandler. They're not all like that."

He shrugged.

"It hasn't been important to me to make friends

with any of them," he said, but he sounded like some-one trying to convince himself of something he really didn't believe in his own heart. "How come you don't have someone steady?"

"Too occupied with my family and my work, I guess. My uncle Peter used to be my escort. He took me everywhere."

"That's the one who was killed recently?"

"Yes."

He nodded.

"Makes you want to stay home and pull the covers over your head," he muttered.

"Yes, exactly."

"Music gets you out. It gets me out, too," he admitted. "That's why I thought you were different from the lollipops. I have a confession to make," he declared.

"What?"

"I noticed you long before Mr. Wengrow suggested we practice together. I pretended I didn't, but I did."

He was quiet, and so was I. He had revealed more than I expected someone like him would already.

"Maybe we'll find more to get us out," I said.

He turned and smiled at me.

When we turned up my driveway, I tried too late to warn him about Grandad Forman's bump. Both our heads nearly hit the ceiling of the car.

"Sorry," I said. "I forgot."

"It's all right. I think. Are my eyes still where they were before I made the turn?"

"Yes," I said, laughing.

When we stopped, Uncle Simon stepped out of the barn and looked our way.

"Wow, he's big."

"He's a very gentle man, Chandler. All those beautiful flowers you see are his doing."

"I guess that's what brings him out."

"Exactly. We all have something."

"You have more," he said. "I'm looking forward to Saturday night."

"Thanks for the ride home. Bye," I said, closing the door.

I watched him back up, turn around, and leave. When I looked at the barn, Uncle Simon was gone, but standing on the porch and looking down at me was Grandad. He looked angry.

"What?" I asked.

"You should be in the henhouse."

"Not this soon, Grandad. I wouldn't have been home this early if I had taken the bus."

"You watch yourself," he warned. He looked in Chandler's direction. "The devil has a pleasing face."

Anyone or anything that does is the devil to you, I wanted to tell him, but I didn't.

Instead, I lowered my head and walked into the

house, away from the fear and the threat that came from his distrusting eyes.

I knew what his trouble was, I thought.

He has nothing to bring him out of the darkness. His only companions were the shadows that lingered in the corners of our home.

I wasn't at all like him. Rather, I hoped and prayed I wasn't. His blood flowed through Daddy's veins and mine, but Grandma Jennie's and Mommy's surely overpowered it.

Or else I would face each dawn with just as much distrust and just as much dreadful expectation.

When he lay his head down for the final sleep, he would finally come out of his darkness only to enter another. That was what loomed ahead for him.

I thought about what Daddy had said about Uncle Peter and Grandad, how Uncle Peter felt more pity for him than he did anger toward him.

He might not like it, but I pitied him, too. Even without Daddy's having told me, I just knew it was better not to let him know.

6

—⁓—

Transformation

I couldn't remember when I was as impatient with the clock as I was waiting for the days to pass until Saturday. Even filling my time with farm chores, homework, and violin practice didn't make those hands move any faster. Chandler was no longer avoiding me at school. The hens had their reason to cackle, but we both avoided them. I learned how to keep my eyes in tunnel vision, something at which Chandler had become expert.

"Why did you lie about you and Chandler?" Karen Jacobs came forward to ask me at the first opportunity. "You were ashamed after all, weren't you?"

"I'm only ashamed of you, Karen. You're so frustrated, you're pathetic," I shot back. Her mouth fell open wide enough to attract flies.

Later, when I told Chandler, he burst into a roar of laughter that drew everyone's attention to us. We were beginning to enjoy our notoriety.

After school on Friday, Daddy took Mommy and me to the mall, where she helped me find a new dress and matching shoes. While we were there, I bought Uncle Simon his birthday present. He was going to be forty-five on Sunday. Mommy had decided to make him dinner and a cake, and had thrown down the gauntlet as soon as Grandad began to utter some opposition. She announced it at dinner Thursday night.

"Making a big thing out of a grown man's birthday is heathen," Grandad started.

"We're going to have a nice party nevertheless," Mommy flared.

I never saw her fill so quickly with what Daddy half-humorously referred to as her Russian fury. The veins in her neck rose against her skin, her shoulders lifted, her hands pressed down on the table, and her eyes looked like they were on springs and would come popping out to shoot across the table at Grandad's face.

Whenever she flew into a high rage, Mommy never turned crimson as much as she developed these two milk-white spots at the corners of her lips. She spoke slowly, taking great care with her words the way someone just practicing the language might. In any case, whatever Grandad Forman saw in her at Thursday night's dinner was enough to close the door quickly on his objections. He shook his head and returned his attention to his food.

Mommy's body slowly receded, losing the swollen shoulders and neck. She threw me a confident smile of satisfaction and talked about her cake. She was planning on making Uncle Simon's favorite: strawberry shortcake.

At the mall I found him a beautiful new set of gardening tools, and then a card specially designed for an uncle. I never called him anything else and never viewed him as a step-uncle, even after I was old enough to understand what that meant. To me he was as much a part of our family as Uncle Peter had been. Love bound us closer than blood.

It had been some time since Mommy and I had gone shopping together. By watching television, she had seen the changes in fashion, but it was still a bit shocking and curious to her. I ended up choosing a round-neck sleeveless shell top in all-over paisley print with shades of fuchsia, burgundy, and black. To wear with it I bought a stretchy, pull-on, knee-length skirt with one-inch ruffle at the hem. To complete the outfit, I chose platform shoes that had crocheted uppers with stretch elastic ankle straps and a ridged sole. Daddy joined us just as I was trying the outfit on, and when I looked back at him standing beside Mommy, I saw an expression of pride on both their faces.

"You look very nice," Daddy said. "Makes you look older."

"Makes her look her age," Mommy corrected. "She's no longer a tomboy farmhand. She's my young lady."

"Mine, too," Daddy said.

"Grandad's not going to like this. He's always saying women are practically naked these days," I said.

"Don't you worry about him," Mommy said, a little of that fury coming back into her eyes. "It's not his business."

She threw Daddy a look, but he turned his eyes away and then said he would bring the car around and meet us at the mall's main entrance.

My heart was thumping with joy and excitement as Mommy and I walked out with my packages piled in my arms. I couldn't help wondering what Chandler would say when he first saw me. Most of my clothing, especially the clothes I wore to school, was so plain and unflattering.

"We'll fix your hair nice, too," Mommy decided.

I smiled to myself, imagining what most of the other girls my age would say or think if their mothers suggested such a thing. I had no fear about Mommy cutting, brushing, and styling my hair for me. Without any sort of formal education, she had come from Russia carrying an unofficial, unwritten degree from the school of common sense and everyday skills. Her grandmothers and her mother had taught her how to cook, create and mend clothes, clean any kind of surface, provide first aid and generally make do with so much less than we had now. They taught her all this before she was ten years old.

What's more, Mommy didn't need Grandad Forman looking over her shoulder to be sure she didn't waste a morsel of food. She knew how to turn leftovers into a fresh new meal. I knew the mothers of my classmates would criticize and ridicule her for being a slave in her own home or something, so I rarely, if ever, bragged about her abilities.

Once, when I had an English assignment to write an essay about someone I considered heroic, I wrote about Mommy. It was before I knew she had come here specifically to marry Daddy without ever having met him. Still, I had often wondered and thought about the courage it had to have taken for someone so young to enter an entirely different world, where people spoke a different language, had different customs and styles, and whole new ways of living. I knew she had come with very little in her possession. What sort of faith in herself did that demand?

Today, my classmates and their mothers moaned and groaned about an hour or so delay at an airport or a traffic jam on a major highway. Girls my age, who were only a year or so younger than Mommy when she had arrived here, thought the world was coming to an end if their CD players broke. The stories they heard about their own grand- and great-grandparents were akin to fables and science fiction. I knew if I told them about Mommy they would look at me as even more of an outsider, weird.

I told them next to nothing.

On Friday night, Mommy worked on my hairdo. She surprised me by having had Daddy buy some recent fashion magazines, so she could study some of the current styles.

"I used to do my mother's hair," she explained after I had washed mine and sat at her small vanity table with a towel over my shoulders. "She handed me a brush when I was no more than five and I would spend hours stroking her hair while she sang or did some needlework. Her hair was the color of dark almonds and she had hazel eyes with tiny green specks. I wondered if I could ever be as beautiful.

"I used to think we would remain forever as we were. I would be forever five and she would be forever a young woman who, when she strolled through our village, wearing that angelic soft smile on her lips, captured the imaginations of every man who saw her, no matter what age. Wives glared angrily at their husbands. I saw it all, walking beside her, holding her hand. I felt like a princess with the queen."

She laughed.

"Why do you laugh, Mommy?"

"Me, thinking I was a princess. We were so poor. My father was a cobbler. He worked very hard to put food on the table. We made use of every crumb, believe me."

"Why did you have to leave Russia, Mommy?" I asked.

"For years my father lived with an imperfect heart. He had a valve problem that, here in America, could be repaired, but we had no money for such a medical procedure. When he died, my mother struggled by taking in other people's wash, mending, doing housework. I was working side by side with her. She aged so quickly it broke my heart."

She stopped working on my hair and stared at herself in the mirror, but I knew she was looking back at a stream of memories instead.

"When I was sixteen, she collapsed one day and was taken to hospital. They said she had to have her gallbladder removed. It was a botched operation in a hospital with poor sanitary conditions. A staph infection was what finally sucked the life out of her. I had to watch the health and beauty drain away every day.

It was almost as if...as if she was evaporating, disappearing right before my eyes.

"One of the last things she said to me was 'Get away from here whenever you can, whatever way you can.'

"I went to live with my aunt."

She took a deep breath.

"The rest you know."

"No, I don't, Mommy. I never knew you came here deliberately to marry Daddy without ever seeing him. How could you do that?"

She smiled.

"Well, I did see a picture of him, but it was a poor picture of a man standing next to a tractor. I thought a man who works with the earth, who makes things grow, has to have a respect for life. I saw kindness in his eyes when we first met, and kindness, my darling daughter, is a rare jewel where I come from, believe me.

"When you look at a young man with whom you think you might become romantic, search for that. Search for a love of living things. You want someone strong, but strong doesn't mean cruel, doesn't mean ruthless. You don't want a conqueror. You want a strong arm around you, yes, but you want soft eyes. You want someone who doesn't love you as a thing possessed, but someone who possesses him."

"How did you get so wise, Mommy?" I asked. I was looking at her in the mirror.

"Pain," she replied. "Unfortunately, that can be the best teacher. But what good is it all if I can't pass the wisdom on to you, my darling daughter? I know your generation is fond of ignoring, even ridiculing their parents and grandparents. I suppose every younger generation is guilty of some of that, but those of you who don't, who take in some of it at least, are far ahead of the others.

"But enough of this serious talk. You're going on a nice date. Let's make you beautiful."

"Can I be beautiful, Mommy?"

"Of course you can. Look at you. You have a face that makes the angels jealous and this hair...it's so rich a miser would choke with envy. I could sell these strands we cut," she kidded. "I should put them in little plastic bags and set up a roadside stand."

I laughed and looked at myself with wonder. Afterward, I thought my mother was truly an artist. When she had finished cutting, blow-drying, and styling my hair, it took my breath away. My whole look had changed. I thought I had suddenly been thrust onto that stage of sophistication I believed belonged only to girls like Susie Weaver. It was as if Mommy had waved a magic wand over my head and turned me from the farm girl with calluses on her hands into Cinderella, ready to go to the ball with her prince.

Would some ugly demon take joy in striking the clock at midnight and turn me back, or would Mommy's magic be too strong even for the evil that Grandad saw looming everywhere in the world around us?

He didn't see me until I sat down for dinner. Before that, I brought Uncle Simon his hot plate. He wasn't waiting at the barn door, so I called to him and started up the stairs. He was sitting under his lamp, trimming a bonsai tree. It was something in which he had just recently become immersed. Mommy had raved so much about his first attempt, he went on to a second and now a third. Grandad thought they were simply silly things, but I saw the way he stared at the two Uncle Simon had given Mommy. He stole looks when he thought no one noticed, but I did, and it brought a smile to my face. If he caught me watching him, he would mutter some ridicule about them again.

"That's beautiful, Uncle Simon," I said. He'd been so intent, it made him jump in his seat.

When he set eyes on me, his mouth opened a little and he just stared. I put his tray on his table.

"What is that one?" I asked.

"What? Oh. It's an incense cedar. Smells good. Here," he said, holding it toward me. I sniffed.

"Yes," I said with delight.

"You look different," he said.

74

"Mommy did my hair. I'm going to a show tomorrow night with my friend Chandler."

"Oh." He looked at his bonsai plant and then at me. "This will be yours," he said. "When it's finished."

"Thanks!"

"It needs music," he warned.

I laughed.

"Okay, Uncle Simon."

"Watching you grow up is the same as watching a flower blossom," he said. He didn't smile or have an impish gleam in his eyes, as some men might when they said such a thing. It was a simple statement from his heart, and it brought tears to my eyes.

"Thank you," I said.

He looked at his food.

"I'd better get back to the house. Grandad hates waiting for anyone when he's ready to eat."

Uncle Simon nodded. I glanced back at him as I left to descend the stairs. He was gazing at me with such a different expression, almost as if he wasn't completely sure I was who I claimed to be, almost as if he wondered if he had seen an apparition.

It's only me, Uncle Simon, I thought. *It's really only me.*

Grandad's reaction was just about what I had expected. He took one look at me and turned to Mommy to declare that I looked like a cheap girl of the streets with my hair cut and styled this way.

"What do you know about such women?" Mommy snapped back at him.

Grandad actually turned a shade darker than beet red.

"I know what I know," he stammered.

"Well, you don't know what is in style and what is not," Mommy said simply and shrugged.

Daddy's lips softened as his eyes turned to her with appreciation.

Grandad looked from one to the other and then at me. He lifted his thick right forefinger.

"Remember. There is no peace, saith the Lord, unto the wicked."

"Beware, old man," Mommy shot back at him, her eyes blazing. "He without sin cast the first stone."

She and Grandad fixed their eyes on each other in such a lock, it took my breath away. I felt an icy hand on my back as the clock ticked.

Then Grandad looked down at his food and Mommy continued serving dinner.

It was the quietest meal I could remember. My ears were filled with the pounding of my heart.

I felt as if I had opened another door in the mansion filled with mysteries when I stepped out of childhood into a woman's world. I had changed right before everyone's eyes.

And soon I would see that they had changed, too.

7

—⚬—

The Wages of Sin

We had no door chimes, no buzzer, only a stem of cast iron with a small ball of iron welded to it to drop against a metal plate. Grandad Forman made it himself. With so few visitors to our home, no one lobbied him to improve upon it. Waiting for Chandler's arrival, I was so nervous it felt like a small army of ants were parading up from my stomach to march around my drum-pounding heart. I debated going downstairs early and sitting by the front window, watching for his car coming up the drive, and then I thought that would look tacky or make me seem too anxious.

Instead, I remained in my room, staring at myself in the mirror, fidgeting with my hair, my clothes, alternating holding my breath with taking deep breaths, and listening hard for the sound of that metal doorknocker reverberating through our hallway. Grandad and Daddy were still out in the west field with Uncle Simon. Mommy was downstairs working on their dinner. I looked at the clock and remembered one of Mommy's favorite expressions: "A watched pot never boils." The hands of the clock indeed looked like they hadn't moved since my last glimpse.

"You're being foolish, Honey," I told myself. "You're acting like a child. It's just a date, just dinner and a show."

Just dinner and a show!

I've never been taken by a boy in my school to dinner and a show, I thought. What was this restaurant he was going to take me to? Would it be some fancy place, where all the other patrons would take one look at me and know I had never been there or anywhere like it before? Would they whisper and smile and laugh at the "girl just off the farm"? And then would they watch my every move to see if I knew which fork to use, did I talk with my mouth open or keep both elbows on the table? Would I eat too much or too little?

Would they laugh at my clothes, my hair, my makeup? Would they know Chandler Maxwell's family and wonder what Chandler was doing with someone so unsophisticated? Would I see all this ridicule in their faces and simply burst out in tears and run from the table?

It was easier milking cows or shoveling chicken manure, I thought.

The metal clang echoing through the house made my heart stop and start. It sounded again, and Mommy called up to me.

"Should I get it for you, Honey?"

"I'm coming," I cried and jumped up. I bounced down the stairs. Mommy came out of the kitchen and stood in the hallway, looking toward the front door. I opened it quickly and stepped back.

Chandler was dressed in a dark blue suit and tie. He looked even more nervous than I was, and for a long moment, neither of us spoke. We just contemplated each other.

"Oh," he said, and brought up a corsage he was holding in his right hand, just behind his leg. "This is for you."

I took it in my hands gently, so gently anyone would have thought it was a newly laid egg.

"Thank you," I said.

Mommy came forward.

"Hello," she said. "You look very handsome," she added.

"Thank you. Honey looks terrific," Chandler said.

"Oh, this is my mother," I leaped to say.

Mommy glanced at me with a laugh on her lips and extended her hand to Chandler.

"How do you do," she said.

"I'm Chandler Maxwell. Pleased to meet you, Mrs. Forman," Chandler said.

"What a beautiful corsage," Mommy said.

I started to fumble with it.

"Here, let me help you do that," Mommy said and fixed it properly. She stepped back. "Very nice. Well, I hope you two have an enjoyable time."

"Thank you," Chandler said. He glanced at me and I stepped forward, walking out with him.

He hurried ahead to open the door for me.

"Thank you," I said and got in.

I looked back at the house. Mommy was in the living room window just between the curtains, peering out at us. I could see the soft smile on her face. Chandler moved around to the driver's side, got in quickly, and started the engine.

"You really do look terrific," he said as we pulled away and down the drive.

"Thank you. Remember the bump!" I cried, and he hit his brake and slowed to go over it.

His laughter broke the film of cellophane we had wrapped around ourselves. I could feel my body relax.

"I hope you like Christopher's. It's close to the theater, so I thought that would be a good choice. You ever been there?" he asked.

"No," I said.

The truth was I had never even heard of it. The only restaurants I had ever gone to were places Uncle Peter had taken me, and they were all more or less restaurant chains, never anything fancy or expensive. Grandad thought eating out was close to a cardinal sin because of the cost.

"It's pretty good. They have a French chef, who's part owner, so he makes a great effort. It's one of my parents' favorite places."

"Oh. Will they be there tonight?" I asked quickly. The thought of that put a dagger of cold fear through my heart.

"No. They have a dinner party at Congressman Lynch's home. That's why my father gave me the tickets. The congressman is in the midst of his big re-election campaign, so he continues to court big political contributions," Chandler added with a smirk. "My mother really enjoys all that glitter. My father has to keep up appearances and mingle. There is a lot of politics involved at the bank. Actually," Chandler said, "there's a lot of politics in practically everything my parents do."

The world he comes from, I thought, *is so different from mine, I would almost feel like Mommy had felt coming from Russia, if I was ever introduced to it.*

"My father says your grandfather's farm is one of the most successful family-run farms in our community," Chandler said. "I didn't get to look around much, but it does look like it's in great shape. I know it's very hard work."

"Very," I said.

"You don't want to become a farmer's wife then, huh?"

"No," I said emphatically and with such conviction, he laughed.

"So, you better practice that violin and get yourself into a good school. Or marry someone very rich," he added.

"If I marry anyone, it won't be because of what he has in his bank account," I replied.

Chandler threw me a look of skepticism.

"I mean that," I said.

"Okay," he said.

When we pulled up to the front of the restaurant, there were young men there to valet park Chandler's car. One of them rushed to open my door, and then another was at the restaurant door to open that for us. I took a deep breath and stepped in alongside Chandler. He approached the hostess, who immediately recognized him and called him, "Mr. Maxwell." She escorted us to our table, a corner booth.

"This is a little more private than the other tables," Chandler explained when we were seated. "I don't like feeling I'm in a fish bowl, do you?"

"Oh, no," I said. He had no idea how grateful I was, being seated where fewer people could observe us.

"I can't get us any wine," he said apologetically.

"That's all right."

The only wine I had ever drunk was a homemade elderberry on Christmas, but I wasn't going to tell him that.

The waiter greeted us, again obviously familiar with Chandler. He handed us the menus, which to my surprise had everything in French. I started to declare my inability to read it, when Chandler turned the page and I saw it was all translated.

"I recommend the duck," Chandler said.

I stared in disbelief at the prices. Everything was à la carte. The only thing they gave us was a platter of bread.

"This is very expensive," I said.

Chandler leaned forward again to whisper.

"I've got my mother's charge card. No problem. Order whatever you want, even caviar, if you want."

"Oh, no," I said quickly. The caviar was more than a hundred dollars itself. "I'll have the duck."

"Good. Me, too," he said, and ordered that for us, and two of what I thought were ridiculously priced salads as well as a large bottle of French water. He told the waiter we were going to a show and the waiter promised to get us served quickly.

I glanced around at some of the other people. The

restaurant was only about a quarter filled. Chandler explained that it was early. The people here were probably all going to the show, too. Everyone was well-dressed, the women in fancy gowns, the men in suits, even tuxedos. I began to worry that I was very underdressed. I didn't have any of the glittering jewelry all the other women had. Chandler misunderstood my looking at everyone with such interest.

"Don't worry," he said confidently, "none of the lollipops are here." He leaned forward and smiled. "It's like flying above bad weather. That's what money does for you."

"Not everyone with less money is bad weather, Chandler," I said.

He shrugged.

"No, not everyone, but enough of them."

"I don't have lots of money," I said.

"Yes," he said, nodding and looking at me firmly, his eyes becoming small and intent as they often did, "but you will, Honey. You will."

"How do you know that?" I asked, smiling.

"I know. I have a built-in wealth detector."

I started to laugh.

"I do!" he insisted.

We were served our salads and talked about the music we were practicing.

"Mr. Wengrow's a bit eccentric," Chandler said, "but I respect his music skills. I've learned a great deal since I've been with him, and he's big enough to admit that he will bring me, and now you, to a point where we'll have to go on to someone more knowledgeable and experienced to improve any more. My parents wanted me to have someone else as a tutor, someone one of their friends had used, but I refused. They thought because Mr. Wengrow was charging far less that he wasn't as good."

"He's the only teacher I've had."

"And look at what wonders he's doing with you," Chandler said quickly.

"Do you really believe that, Chandler?"

"I'm not in the habit of saying things I don't believe," he replied.

I smiled at him, this time not so displeased with his arrogant tone.

The waiter arrived with our main dishes and we began to eat.

I was impressed with the duck, and had to admit that I had only eaten wild duck my mother had prepared.

"We still have time for dessert," Chandler said, checking his watch. "What about a crème brûlée?" he suggested. "They really make a great one here."

I had never had one before, of course, and didn't even know what was in it.

"I guess," I said.

When it came and I took a taste, I was unable to hide my pleasure and surprise.

"First time you had that?" he asked.

"Yes. It's so delicious," I declared, and he laughed.

"I knew it would be fun being with you," he said. "I'm glad you said yes."

"I am, too."

I was able to glance at the bill. Grandad Forman would have exploded at the table, I thought. He would yell that he could buy another cow for that.

When we arrived at the theater, there were valets to park the car there, too. I was surprised and pleased at our seats. They were practically on the stage. Contrary to what Chandler suspected, the show was wonderful. Afterward we both raved about the leads and the quality of the music.

All the way back to the farm, we talked incessantly, leaping in on each other's momentary pauses as if we were terrified of silence. As we approached the driveway, Chandler slowed down to nearly a crawl.

"I'm sorry," he said. "I should have asked you if you wanted to go somewhere else first."

"That's all right. I couldn't eat anything else," I said.

"Your big uncle going to be waiting at the door?" he asked.

"He might be," I said, laughing.

Chandler brought the car to an abrupt stop.

"Then I better kiss you good night right here," he said and leaned over to kiss me. It was a quick kiss, almost a snap of lips. He knew how disappointing it was even without my saying anything. "Not too good, huh?"

"Let's say you're better at playing the piano."

He laughed, hesitated, and came toward me again. This time the kiss was longer and hard enough to start my heart tapping and bring a warmth up my body. He held himself close.

"You're the prettiest, nicest girl in the school, Honey. I've got to thank Mr. Wengrow."

"He might not understand why," I said, and Chandler laughed.

"No, he might not." He sat back. "Sure you don't want to go somewhere else?"

I looked up the driveway. I knew Mommy and Daddy were waiting up for me, and Uncle Simon was most probably sitting by his window, too.

"Not tonight," I said. "But I had a great time. I really did. Thank you," I said.

"Okay," he said, his voice dripping with disappointment. He started up the driveway. "Bump away," he cried, and we laughed as we went over Grandad's hump in the road.

I didn't see Uncle Simon anywhere when we pulled up. His room looked dark, too. I did see a curtain move in the living room.

"Looks quiet here," Chandler said. "I could have gotten away with a good night kiss after all."

"It's not too late," I said.

He smiled in the dim pool of light coming off our single, naked porch bulb. Then he slid closer to me, put his arm around my shoulder, and brought his lips to mine again, stronger, longer, full of passion.

"Just takes practice," I said. "Like the piano."

He laughed loudly.

"I really like you, Honey. You don't beat around the bush or pretend to be someone you're not. You're fun to be with. I mean it."

"I'm glad," I said and started to open the car door. He got out quickly and ran around to finish opening it for me.

"Miss Forman," he said with a mock bow. "We hope you enjoyed yourself tonight."

"Indeed I did, sir."

He walked me to the front steps, said good night again, and got back into his car. I watched him back away and then I waved to him, and he waved back and started down the driveway.

"You let that boy touch your body sinfully?" I heard, and spun around to see Grandad step out of a deep shadow to the right of the front porch.

"Grandad, you frightened me."

"Remember, the wages of sin is death. Remember."

"I didn't sin," I flared. "I didn't do anything wrong."

"I saw you," he said, stepping into the perimeter of the light. "I saw you in the car."

"It's not a sin to kiss someone good night, Grandad."

"One thing leads to another," he said. He pointed his finger at me. "God knows what lust lies in your heart. You'll bring His wrath upon us all," he declared.

"I will not," I said. "That's a silly thing to say."

"You were too close with Peter," he suddenly said. It took my breath away.

"What? What's that supposed to mean?"

"I watched the two of you. The Lord saw what was in both your hearts and struck him down."

"That's a horrible thing to say, Grandad. How can you say such a horrible thing? You're terrible! I hate you for saying something as terrible as that."

"Don't be insolent," he threatened and took a step toward me.

"Leave her be," we heard. I turned to see Uncle Simon coming out of the barn.

"Go on with you," Grandad said, waving at him.

The front door opened and Mommy stepped out. She took one look at Grandad, another at me, and then at Uncle Simon.

"What's going on out here?" she demanded.

Instead of replying, I put my head down and ran up the stairs, past her and into the house. Daddy was in the hallway, a look of surprise on his face, too.

"Honey?"

I shook my head, the tears flying off my cheeks,

and charged up the stairs into my room and slammed the door shut.

Thank God Chandler had driven away when he had.

I didn't put on the light in my room. I simply threw myself on my bed and pressed my face into the pillow. Grandad's horrible words circled me like insistent mosquitos, biting and stinging. How could he harbor such ugly thoughts in his mind? How could he turn something that had been gentle and kind, loving and beautiful, into the most detestable and ugly ogre of smut and filth? He made me feel dirty inside and out. I shook my body as if to throw off the stains.

What had he been doing all those years while I was growing up and Uncle Peter was at my side, taking my hand, showing me wonderful things in nature, swinging me about, hugging me, kissing me, and lavishing gifts on me? Was he hiding somewhere in the shadows, watching us, forming these disgusting thoughts? The day Uncle Peter was killed, did he actually look at me and think I was somewhat responsible?

I started to sob when I heard my door open and close softly. I stopped, took a breath, and turned. Mommy was standing there, her back against the door. The moonlight illuminated her face. For a moment it looked like a mask, her eyes were so dark and deep.

"What did he say to you, Honey?" she asked softly.

I scrubbed the tears out of my eyes with my fists and sat up, taking a breath before speaking, not knowing if I could even form the words in my mouth.

"He said I was too close with Uncle Peter and because of that God struck him down."

Mommy said something in Russian under her breath.

"He's a sick, twisted old man. You must not pay any attention to him."

"I can't look at him," I said.

Mommy came over and sat beside me. She patted my hand and stroked my hair.

"Did you have a good time with Chandler?"

"Yes, a wonderful time. He spent a lot of money on dinner, too."

She laughed.

"When I was a young girl, my mother used to tell me to find a man who is frugal, who won't waste a ruble on you because, in the end, you'll have security."

"Chandler's family is very rich, Mommy. They can waste money and still have security."

She laughed again.

"Why is Grandad Forman so mean? Why would he say such a thing to me now?"

"He's coming to the end of his life and looking back on his own sins," she said. "He's trying to win back God's sympathies. He thinks he's Job from the

Bible. He likes suffering because he thinks it gives him a chance to show God how faithful he is."

"What sins are in his past? He lives like a monk or something," I said.

"No man is perfect, especially not your grandfather. Forget what he said. He's like some creature eating out its own heart. I won't let him say anything like that to you again," she vowed.

"How can you stop him, Mommy? He owns everything. He never stops reminding us."

"He owns nothing," she said and stood up. "Go to sleep thinking about the nice things that happened tonight. Tell yourself your grandfather wasn't even there."

"I thought Uncle Simon was going to get into a fight with him. I was so frightened."

"I know. Don't think about it," she repeated. She walked to the door.

"Practice your violin, Honey. Do well in school. I'll tell you what my mother told me. Find a way to leave this place," she added, then opened the door and left me sitting in the darkness, wondering what she had not said.

In my heart I knew it would come; it would come soon.

8

—∞—

Making Beautiful Music

Despite his constant Bible-thumping and hell and damnation speeches, Grandad Forman was not a churchgoing man. In fact, he was highly critical of organized religion, calling it just another exploitation and therefore another playground for the devil. Mommy chastised him for this, especially on Sunday when she, Daddy, and I would get dressed up and go to church. Uncle Simon was too shy about meeting people and being out in public, and Mommy never pressured him, but she and Grandad often argued about his refusal to attend the Lord's house of worship.

"I don't need no preacher to tell me what God wants of me and what He don't," Grandad insisted.

"You need to bow your head in the house of the Lord more than any of us," Mommy threw back at him.

Their eyes locked and Grandad left the room or walked away, mumbling to himself. He did spend his early Sunday time alone, reading his Bible, the pages of which were worn so thin, the edges were torn and yellow. From the time I was a little girl on, I was always fascinated by the way he gripped it in his hand, holding it tightly between his thumb and fingers as he would the handle of a hatchet or a hammer, sometimes waving it at one of us, especially Uncle Simon. When he did, Grandad's eyes were always brightened, luminous and shiny, resembling stones in a brook. After seeing Star Wars, I had a dream in which I saw a ray of light come out of Grandad's Bible, which he wielded like a sword over us all, even Uncle Simon.

Every Sunday, after I returned from church and changed into my jeans, I would hurry out to help Uncle Simon weed his garden and tend to his plants. This Sunday I was very excited because I was going to give him his birthday present. Mommy had already told him about our special dinner, after which we would have his birthday cake. I found him on his knees, working around a patch of ginger lilies. Everything I knew about flowers, I knew because of Uncle Simon.

It was a particularly beautiful late spring day with

a breeze as gentle as a soft kiss caressing my face. Against the western sky, I saw a string of clouds so thin they looked like strips of gauze. A flock of geese in their perfect V-formation were making their way farther north. *What a wonderful day for a birthday,* I thought.

As I approached Uncle Simon, I could hear him muttering lovingly to his flowers. It brought a smile to my face. As if he had known where my uncle Simon was this morning, the minister had preached about a respect for life and how that gave us a deeper appreciation of ourselves, our own souls, and God's precious gifts.

"Happy birthday, Uncle Simon," I said, and he turned quickly and looked up at me, his bushy eyebrows lifting like two sleeping caterpillars. He looked from me to the gift box in my hands, and then wiped his hands on the sides of his jeans and stood up.

"What's that?" he asked.

"Your birthday present." I thrust it toward him. "From me, Mommy, and Daddy," I said. I wasn't going to include Grandad, not only because he didn't contribute to it, but because he ridiculed birthdays.

Uncle Simon took the box so gently in his large hands, I smiled.

"It's nothing breakable," I said.

He stood there, gazing down at it, looking overwhelmed by the fancy wrap.

"Open it," I urged, anxious to see his reaction to the gift.

He looked at me and nodded. He tried taking the paper off carefully, but it tore and he looked disappointed in himself. Then he opened the box and gazed at the new garden tools.

"Ooooh," he said, stretching his expression of pleasure as if he was peering down at some of the world's most precious jewels. "Good. Thank you, Honey."

I smiled and stepped forward, lifting myself on my toes to kiss him on the cheek.

"Happy birthday, Uncle Simon."

He nodded and took out the tools, turning them around and inspecting each more closely.

"They're almost too pretty to use," he said. He gazed at his old, rusted, crudely made ones as if he was about to say a final good-bye to an old, dear friend.

"It'll make your flowers happier," I said.

He smiled.

"Yes, it might," he agreed and turned to scrape away some weeds.

I got down beside him and we worked in silence for a while. His garden was growing so well and was so large now, people came around to see it and offer to buy flowers from him. He cherished every plant so much, he was at first reluctant to give any up, but Mommy convinced him by telling him he was giving the flowers added life through the pleasure and enjoyment others took in them. He would have done most anything Mommy asked him to do anyway, I thought.

When Grandad Forman saw that he was beginning to make some significant money with his flowers, he told Uncle Simon he had to give him a percentage for the use of the land. Uncle Simon would have given him all of it, but Mommy stood between them like a broker and negotiated Grandad down to ten percent. She found out what a fair price was for each of the flowers, too. Recently, Daddy had brought up the idea of making a regular nursery, investing in a greenhouse.

"It would be a profitable side business," he declared.

"I can't see putting any real money behind him," Grandad said.

"Why not?" Mommy challenged. "Has he ever failed to do something you asked him to do? Has he ever neglected his chores?"

"He's got the brain of a child," Grandad insisted.

Mommy straightened her shoulders and gazed down at him with eyes so full of fire and strength, both Daddy and I were mesmerized.

"The wolf also shall dwell with the lamb, and the leopard shall lie down with the kid; and the calf and the young lion and the fatling together; and a little child shall lead them," she recited.

"You don't have to quote Scripture to me,"

Grandad cried, the lines in his face deepening as he stretched his lips in anger. His leather-tan skin looked as stiff as the crust of stale bread.

"Seems I do from the things you say. And," she added softly, "things you do."

He looked at her and then looked away.

"Do what you want," he muttered, "but not with any money of mine."

It was still a secret, but Daddy was seriously looking into the greenhouse idea.

"Who taught you how to grow flowers so well, Uncle Simon?" I asked him as I worked with him.

He paused and looked toward the house as if he actually saw someone standing there.

"Your grandma," he said. "I worked with her in her garden. It was the only place and time she had any peace," he added, a shaft of embittered light passing through his dark eyes. He dug a little more aggressively for a moment, and then his body relaxed and he went back to his calm manner.

I watched him, admiring how he drifted into a rhythm, how he and his work seemed to flow together, his face full of pleasure and contentment, and I thought about what Uncle Peter had said about me and my violin.

The flowers play Uncle Simon, I thought. They nurture him. They rip the weeds away from him. They turn his face to the sunlight and the rain.

That evening, looking as clean and well-dressed as he could, he came to the house. Daddy gave him another present: his favorite aftershave lotion, which had a flowery scent. Mommy had prepared a turkey dinner with all the trimmings. It was as good as our Thanksgiving. Grandad Forman muttered about the cost of such a meal just for a grown man's birthday, but ate vigorously nevertheless. Then Mommy brought out the cake.

"I couldn't put all the candles on the cake, Simon," Mommy explained, "so I just lit the one to represent them all."

He laughed and blew it out. We all sang "Happy Birthday." Grandad almost moved his lips, but shook his head as if to deny his own inclinations. Afterward, we sat in the living room and I played my violin for Uncle Simon. As usual, I became lost in my melodies, feeling as though the violin was a part of me, as if my very being flowed into it and out in the form of music.

Toward the end of my little concert, I opened my eyes and looked at them all. What surprised and even put a titter of anxiety in my heart was the way Grandad Forman was looking at me. Gone from his face was any expression of disdain or disapproval. For a moment he looked like any warm and loving grandparent might, sitting there and listening to his grandchild perform. It confused me, but I was sure I saw something deeper in him. I wanted to call it love, but I was afraid to think that. Toward the end, I caught the way he glanced at Mommy and how that changed his expression, restoring his cold, impersonal manner.

"Time to go to sleep," he declared after Mommy, Daddy, and Uncle Simon gave me their applause. He rose and walked out of the room.

"Thank you," Uncle Simon said.

"Many more birthdays, Simon," Mommy told him and gave him a hug and a kiss.

Daddy patted him on the shoulder.

I walked out with him and stood on the front porch, watching him cross the yard toward the barn. Daddy came out and stood beside me.

"How can this be enough for him, Daddy?" I asked. "How can he really be happy?"

"I guess it's a matter of finding your own way, making peace with that part of yourself that's usually demanding more, that lusts after things others have and makes you discontented with what you have," Daddy said.

"You make it sound bad to want more, Daddy. Isn't it good to be ambitious?"

"Sure, but when it keeps you looking over at the next field, you never enjoy what you've accomplished, what you've grown on your own. That's too much ambition, I guess."

"How do you know when it's too much, when you should stop?" I asked.

He shook his head.

"It's different for everyone, Honey. Something inside you has to cry out, enough!"

"Has that happened to you?"

He smiled at me and put his arm around my shoulders.

"Yes," he said, "and now, I can watch you go for it."

"Like Uncle Simon watches his flowers emerge from the seeds he planted?"

"Yes."

"And like Grandad watched you and Uncle Peter?"

"Something like that," Daddy said, but his arm lost its tightness and his eyes shifted away. It was as if he was suddenly searching the shadows for signs of one of Grandad's demons.

"I better get to bed," he told me. "We've got work to do tomorrow."

He left me on the porch, looking into the darkness and then up at Uncle Simon's room. The light went out there, too, and I suddenly felt a chill. I don't know where it came from. There was barely a breeze and the night was warm.

It came from inside me, I concluded.

It came from the sense of some terrible secret still looming above me, masked, disguised, hidden behind the eyes of those who loved me and those who knew and were stirred by the same wintry feeling creeping in and over all our smiles and all our laughter, and even into our dreams.

The following week, Chandler and I officially became an item at our school. We were together everywhere we could be together. The joy we were taking in each other's company quickly became apparent, and soon I detected the looks of envy in the eyes of girls who were still searching for someone. I also noticed that Chandler was far less defensive with and suspicious of other students. The relaxation that was evident in his face took form in the way he dressed as well. He started coming to school in far less formal clothing; his hair wasn't as plastered and stiff, and he was joking and laughing with other students more often than before.

"We took a vote," Susie Weaver told me after lunch on Friday, "and decided you've been a good influence on Chandler Maxwell. He's almost a human being now."

"Thank you so much for your compliments," I said with a cold smile. "It is a coincidence."

"What? Why?"

"Chandler and I were wondering when you were going to become a human being," I replied, and left her with her mouth open wide enough to attract a whole hive of bees.

That afternoon Chandler asked me to go to a movie with him. He thought we should go have something to eat first, too, but said it wouldn't be any fancy restaurant.

"Let's just have a pizza or something," he suggested. "To celebrate our continued musical success."

We had pleased Mr. Wengrow at our duet lessons on Wednesday night. Chandler had come to the house to pick me up and take me there. I saw the look of both pleasure and surprise in Mr. Wengrow's face.

All he said about it was, "I'm happy you're both getting along so well. It shows in your work."

We exchanged conspiratorial smiles and worked with new enthusiasm.

"I know that Chandler is all set as far as his continuing education goes," Mr. Wengrow said at the end of our session, while I was putting my violin in its case, "but you're still not decided, is that correct?"

"No," I said. "My parents and I talked about my attending the community college and living at home."

"There's no music program there that will add to your ability and talent in any significant way," he said quickly. "I don't mean to interfere, but I think you've got what it takes to get into a prestigious school for the performing arts. I'll speak with your parents, of course, but I wanted to talk to you about it first."

I looked at Chandler, who shrugged and smiled.

"What school? Where?"

"I have a good friend who is actually the accountant for a theatrical agent. I would like to contact him to see if he would do me a favor and get an audition arranged for you."

"Oh," I said. "Where?"

"New York City," Mr. Wengrow said.

"New York City!"

All I could think of was Grandad Forman's ravings about the twin cities of iniquity being Los Angeles and New York. He called them both cities built by Satan, and loved to point his finger at the television screen whenever some horrible crime or event was reported occurring in either of them.

"There!" he would cry. "See what I mean?"

"If you're going to do anything significant in the arts, you should be in New York City," Mr. Wengrow said.

I shook my head.

"I don't think my parents would like that, Mr. Wengrow."

"I'll have a word with them," he said. "Don't worry. I'll get them to understand."

Chandler was going to the Boston University School of Arts. His father was an alumnus of BU and a heavy contributor, not that Chandler couldn't get in on his own ability.

"Mr. Wengrow's right," he told me afterward.

"You'll smother to death here. You've got to get out and into the big wide world."

It made me very nervous to think about it, so I didn't, and up until the following weekend, Mr. Wengrow had not spoken about it with my parents. If he had, he might have been very discouraged and not mentioned the discussion to me at all, I thought.

On Friday, Chandler drove up to take me to the movies. I had put on a mustard-colored light sweater and a pair of jeans with a pair of high-heel sneakers I had managed to get Mommy to buy me, despite how silly she thought they looked. She couldn't understand why they were the rage. I had my hair tied in a ponytail.

"You look like Debbie Reynolds in one of those old movies," Chandler declared as soon as he saw me come bounding down the front steps. "I love it."

"Thank you."

He was wearing a black mock turtleneck shirt, which brought out the dark color in his eyes. I thought he looked very sexy, and practically leaped into the car to sit beside him. I couldn't remember when I had been happier.

As we started away, Grandad came out of nowhere onto the driveway and stood in the wash of Chandler's car headlights. His gray hair looked like it was on fire, his eyes blazing at us. Chandler hit the brake pedal and I gasped.

"Who's that?" he cried.

"My grandad," I said.

"Well, what's he doing?"

Grandad simply stood there in our way, staring at us. Suddenly he raised his right hand, and I saw he was holding his sacred old Bible. He held it up like some potential victim of a vampire would hold up a cross in a horror movie, and then he stepped to the side and disappeared into the shadows.

Chandler turned to me, amazed.

"What was that all about?"

"Just drive," I said, choking back my tears. Chandler stared at me. "Drive, Chandler, please."

"Sure," he said and accelerated, taking the bump too hard.

I curled up into a ball. I was filled with a mixture of anger and fear. No matter how Mommy stood up to him, I couldn't help but be intimidated by his accusing eyes. Memories of him coming into my room when I was a little girl abounded. I saw him standing over my bed, chanting his prayers, reciting his biblical quotes, giving me warnings about hell, sin, and damnation that I was still too young to understand. What I did understand was there was some sort of danger awaiting me should I do anything defiant.

"What was that in his hand?" Chandler finally asked. "Honey?"

I took a deep breath and emerged slowly, like a clam opening its shell.

"His Bible," I said.

"Bible? Why was he holding it up?"

"To remind me that the wages of sin is death," I said in a tired, defeated voice.

"Sin? What sin?"

"The sin he thinks I'm about to commit," I said.

Chandler was very quiet. Then he looked at me, shook his head and smiled.

"The movie is only rated PG-13."

I looked at him, and then we both laughed. It felt like balm on a wound. He reached out to touch my hand, and I slid closer to him.

"I've got to admit, he scared me," Chandler said. "I couldn't imagine who or what he was, jumping out into the drive like that."

"Let's not talk about it anymore," I begged.

"Okay," he said, eagerly agreeing.

At the pizza restaurant, we talked about some of the other students at school, our classes, and Mr. Wengrow. Chandler's theory was that because he had no children, he put fatherly concern into us and saw himself as a surrogate father, giving us guidance.

"Sometimes, I feel like he cares more about me than my own father," Chandler admitted. "I mean, my dad wants me to succeed and all, but he doesn't have the same interest in my music or faith in what I can do with it. He's always talking to me about becoming a lawyer or going to medical school, as if nothing else has any reason to be. I get the distinct feeling he's paying for my lessons just to humor me, almost like putting up with a nuisance."

"What about your mother?" I asked.

"She usually goes along with anything he says. She's busy at being busy."

"What's that mean?" I asked, smiling.

"She makes work for herself. No one appreciates the fax machine as much as my mother. She lives off the papers that all the organizations, volunteers, and people send her, and then she spends hours filing, organizing meaningless things. She's content as long as her name is on every possible list of patrons and committee lists, whether she actually does anything for the cause or not.

"It's like she lives in a castle built out of cards, or invitations to charity functions, I should say. She's turned it into her own cottage industry."

He sounded so bitter about it.

"You're upset about all that?"

He stared at his piece of pizza for a moment and then shook his head.

"Sometimes, I wish I was a charity instead of a son. I'd get more attention. What about your parents? Do they care about your music?"

I told him about Uncle Peter and how Daddy had become more and more committed to my playing.

"They should let you go to a good school then," he

said. "I hope Mr. Wengrow can convince them. You have something, Honey. You can be someone."

"So can you," I said quickly.

"I don't know. Maybe."

"Why maybe?"

"I don't have as much passion as you do. I'm good, technically very good, I know, but there's one other thing that makes the difference, and you have it," he said, his eyes fixed on my face. "I envy you for that."

"You've got it, too," I insisted.

He smiled.

"Maybe if I keep hanging around with you, it will rub off or I'll catch it, like a cold," he said. "Of course, we have to get closer and closer before that might happen."

"That's okay with me."

We stared at each other. I felt my heart begin to pound, the warm glow rise from just under my breasts, up my neck, and into my face.

"We can go to a different movie tonight," he said.

"What do you mean?"

"My parents are out for the evening. I have a great DVD collection. You ever see a DVD movie?"

"I don't even know what it is."

"You've got to see it," he said excitedly. "I have about fifty movies. You can choose any one you want. You'll think you're in the movie theater. Okay?"

He waved to the waitress for our check.

I felt as though I had stepped into the ocean and was being pulled out to sea with the outgoing tide. There was no way to resist. It was best to simply relax and go along.

Chandler's house was a large, stone-wall-clad Tudor with a circular driveway set on a grand track of prime land just outside our small city. From the well-trimmed hedges and bushes to the immaculate sidewalk and rich dark oak front doors, his house looked elegant enough to be the home of a governor. I was awed by the size of the entryway, the marble floors, and elaborate chandeliers. All of the furniture looked brand-new and expensive.

"C'mon," he said eagerly after we had entered. He took my hand and rushed me along past the large dining room, in which I glimpsed the longest table I had ever seen, dressed with place settings and silver dishes as if a gala evening was about to commence.

He brought me to what he called their media room. There was a television set so big it nearly rivaled some of the smaller-screen movie theaters.

"Dad's always competing with his friends when it comes to state-of-the-art equipment," he explained. "Wait until you hear the sound system."

He opened a dark mahogany wood closet to reveal a collection of movies that looked like it contained anything and everything ever made.

"Choose," he commanded.

I shook my head.

"I don't know where to begin."

"Whatever you want," he said. "Don't worry about the ratings either," he said, winking.

I glanced at him and then at the titles. I really didn't know which one to pick.

"You choose," I said.

"Okay. This is one of my favorites," he said. "Sit on the settee," he added, nodding toward it.

I sat and waited for him to get it started. Everything was on a remote, even the room's lights. He dimmed them and sat beside me. The movie began, and it was everything he had described. I did feel as if we were in a theater.

"Incredible, huh?"

"Yes," I said.

"We can even have popcorn, if you want."

"I'm still stuffed with pizza."

"Me, too. Want to drink something? Anything?" he said impishly.

"I'm fine," I said.

He nodded and we sat back to watch the movie. I felt his arm move around my shoulders and then his hand against my side, pulling me closer to him. His lips were on my cheek, soon moving up to kiss my hair.

"We're not going to see much of this movie if you

do that," I said. When I turned to him, he was only an inch or so from me.

His response was to kiss me on the lips and hold me tighter.

"Pretend we're in an old drive-in movie," he whispered.

"I've never been in one," I said.

"Me neither, but we can pretend, can't we?"

"I don't know."

"I do," he said. He kissed me again, moving his lips down to my neck. "I really like you, Honey. No one makes me feel as comfortable and happy as you do."

I said nothing. His words, his warm touch, the power of his eyes were quickly sweeping away any tenseness I had. I felt myself soften in his arms and wanted to kiss him as hard and as passionately as he was kissing me. When his hand grazed my breast, I tightened.

"It's all right," he said. "If you like me as much as I like you, it's all right."

My heart was pounding. The tingle that traveled up and down my spine and swirled in around my heart was delightful, warm, welcome. His fingers went under my sweater and moved quickly up to my breast. When he touched me, he brought his lips down on mine harder. His tongue moved between my lips. We were sliding down on the leather settee and he was moving over me. He had lifted the edge of my bra cup and touched my naked breast. It seemed like thunder in my head, my blood was rushing so fast around my body.

"I think I love you, Honey. I can't imagine liking someone as much as I like you without it being love," he continued, whispering in my ear.

"Like the serpent whispered into Eve's ear," I heard Grandad say.

Chandler's right hand moved down behind my shoulder and under my sweater. His fingers and palm traveled like a hungry spider up to my bra clip, which he squeezed and undid so quickly, I barely had a chance to shake my head. My bra lifted and a moment later, his left hand was over my breast. I was breathing so hard and fast, I thought I would faint.

There were feelings being born everywhere along my legs and in the pit of my stomach, feelings I had tempted and taunted in dreams. My own rush of pleasure was sweeping over me like the wave I imagined myself caught in earlier. I could feel the great struggle going on inside me, the battle between the forces that wanted me to push him away and jump up and the forces that wanted me to soften, relax, fall back, and invite him to go further and further.

"You do love me, too, don't you, Honey? Don't you?" he pleaded, lifting my sweater so he could bring his lips to my breasts.

I opened my eyes. I wanted to say yes. I wanted to

speak, but I suddenly imagined Grandad standing there looking down at us, nodding. He extended his arm to put his Bible on Chandler's back, and I screamed.

Frightened by my cry, Chandler pulled himself away. The image of Grandad evaporated instantly, popping like a bubble.

"What's wrong?" Chandler asked.

I caught my breath and sat up.

"I'm sorry," I said. "I couldn't..."

Chandler slumped against the settee.

"Don't you like me enough, Honey?"

"Yes, I just...couldn't, Chandler."

"Why not?"

"I couldn't," I repeated and fixed my bra. "I'm sorry," I said.

"Me, too," he said, looking petulant and crabby. "We probably should have just gone to the movie theater."

"I said I was sorry, Chandler."

"When you wanted to come here, I thought you wanted to be with me."

"I do," I insisted.

"Right."

"I've never done this before," I confessed. He looked at me, and then at the floor. "I thought you knew that, too."

"I'm not exactly Don Juan myself," he said.

"What I felt, what I hoped, was that when the right girl came along, a girl who thought I was the right guy," he added, turning back to me, "we'd trust each other enough to...to love each other."

I felt tears coming to my eyes.

"I trust you and I *want* to love you," I said. "But..."

"But?"

"You didn't just sit at your piano and start playing Mozart's Concerto in A Major, did you?"

He stared at me a moment.

"It's not something you need to practice to get right. At least, I don't think of it that way," he said.

"But it's not something to rush into, either. It's not practice. It's building a relationship, learning to care and care for each other until you both feel ready for all of it," I said. "Too many girls I know don't think it's anything special anymore. Am I wrong?"

"No," he said. He smiled. "Okay," he said. "I'm sorry."

I sat back, and we both turned to the movie once again.

But out of the corner of my eye, I looked to the doorway. I searched every shadow.

I was looking for Grandad.

9

—⚬—

The Pond

Chandler and I enjoyed the remainder of the movie and then sat and talked for nearly an hour afterward. We had just started out when the front door opened and his parents came in, quite unaware that Chandler had brought anyone to their home. I knew that was true because they were arguing quite vehemently as they entered, his father complaining about his mother's ridiculous infatuation with the Ivers, who he said were perfect examples of the nouveau riche, people who had inherited money and had no class.

"This," he declared before either of them glanced our way, "is a perfect example of why clothes do *not* make the man. An oaf in a tuxedo is still an oaf, and

I'm surprised that you, of all people, can't see that, Amanda."

"I am not infatuated with anyone. I'm merely... oh," Chandler's mother moaned, grimacing so emphatically she made her face look like a rubber mask, stretching her lips and widening her eyes when she saw the two of us standing there, listening to them.

She was otherwise an attractive woman, stately, her black hair perfectly cut and styled. She wore a thin wrap with fur cuffs and a collar, and diamond earrings hung in gold leaves glittered under the hallway chandelier's light. When she turned and her wrap opened, I saw the biggest diamond pendant I had ever seen in real life, lying softly just above her cleavage, prominently displayed in her deep V-neck satin gown.

Chandler's father was dressed in a tuxedo with a vibrantly red silk scarf over his shoulders. I guess dapper was the proper word for him. I saw the great resemblance between Chandler and him, especially around their eyes and their mouths. However, Chandler's nose was smaller and straighter, and I thought he had a stronger chin. They were about the same height.

"What's this?" he asked, a look of annoyance disrupting his face. It was as if Chandler had brought home a prostitute or something. At least, that was the way he made me feel when he fixed his critical eyes on me.

"Dad," Chandler said, not losing a bit of his cool, calm demeanor, "Mom, I'd like you to meet Honey Forman, the girl I told you about, the one who plays the violin and practices with me once a week," he added, obviously annoyed it was taking both of them so long to recall my name and who I was. "At Mr. Wengrow's house? Remember?"

"Oh," his mother said, jumping as if someone had touched her behind with one of Grandad's cattle prods. "Yes, of course." She scrunched her nose and wrinkled the area around her eyes as she peered at me. "You two weren't practicing your music now, were you?"

"I doubt that," his father said, giving her a look that practically shouted "stupid."

"Oh," his mother said again. "Then what..."

"I brought Honey here to see our new television system and watch a movie on it," Chandler explained.

"New television system?"

"He's talking about the DVD player, new widescreen television set, and the surround sound system I recently had installed, Amanda," his father said.

"Oh." She looked very confused.

"I wonder why it doesn't surprise me that you've forgotten about it," his father said.

"Well, you know I don't watch very much television these days, Dalton."

"Right."

"We were just on our way out," Chandler said. "I'm taking Honey home."

"Forman. Right, yes. Your grandfather is Abraham Forman, the Forman farm," Chandler's father said, as if he was giving me the information for the first time. "It's one of the more successful family-run farms these days," he told Chandler's mother. "It's an immaculate property, a jewel in our community," he added. "The farmer is still a large part of the backbone of this country," he lectured.

"How nice," Chandler's mother said. "I'm sorry I can't stand here and chat, but I must get out of these clothes and relax, Chandler. We didn't have an enjoyable evening," she said, "and I'd just like to forget about it as quickly as I can. Nice to have met you..." She looked at Chandler. "I'm sorry, did you say her name was Honey or did you call her honey?"

"That's my name, Mrs. Maxwell," I said.

"Is it? How...different. Well, nice to have met you anyway," she said and walked toward the stairs.

Chandler moved quickly to open the front door for me. He and his father exchanged angry looks, and we started out.

"Good night, Mr. Maxwell," I said. "It was nice to meet you, too."

Chandler closed the door sharply behind us before his father could reply.

"Sorry about their being so stuffy," he said as we walked to his car.

"I guess they were just taken by surprise," I said.

He nodded, but after we started away, he said it wasn't just their being surprised.

"I wish I could blame it on that, but I'm afraid my parents are somewhat snobby. They both come from wealthy families and rarely have gone anywhere in their lives that wasn't first class. All their friends are just like them," he continued. "I'm like you, Honey. I need to get away, too. Especially from that," he tagged on.

"What are you looking for, Chandler?" I asked him, wondering what he meant by "like you."

How could I not wonder how he and I were alike? The worlds we came from were so vastly different. Most of the young people our age would and even did envy him for what he had already. I remembered Daddy's comments about people who were always looking beyond their own fields of achievement, their own accomplishments, yearning to have what someone else had. Was Chandler one of them? Would he ever be happy?

He was quiet for a long moment. Then he smiled to himself and turned to me.

"Remember that night after our first duet practice,

when you told me if I understood how the piano plays me, I'd understand myself, and I countered by saying who says I don't understand myself?"

"Yes," I said.

"Well, I was just being a big shot, Honey. I don't know who I am. I think I'm on the bottom of the list when it comes to that. I mean, I should have no problem with identity. My parents put our name out there prominently. Everyone knows who I am but me.

"Parents take it for granted that because you have inherited their name and because you walk in the long, wide shadows they cast, you'll be just another example of who they are and what they are. My parents can't even begin to imagine me not being happy with the things that make them happy.

"Somehow, parents take it personal if you claim your own identity, set out to be different. They see it as a rejection of them, but it's not that. It's a search for your own self-meaning.

"That's what I have to discover and that's why I have to get away."

He grimaced.

"Sorry," he said. "I didn't mean to get so deep and lay all this heavy stuff on you."

"No, I'm glad you did."

"Really? Most girls would just think me very boring, I'm sure," he said.

"You're hardly that, Chandler."

He smiled.

"I am without you," he said.

He reached for my hand and I snuggled closer to him. We were silent, moving along, the headlights of his car plowing a path through the darkness for us, both of us wondering what really lay ahead.

He drove very slowly up our driveway, probably expecting Grandad to pop out at us from some dark shadow again. I was half-expecting something like that myself. To both our reliefs, there was no one around. It was quiet and dark. Uncle Simon's light was off and so were most of the lights in my house.

"I had a good time, Honey," Chandler said. "I hope you did, too," he added, a worried look in his eyes.

"I did," I said convincingly enough to bring a smile back to his face.

"I'll call you tomorrow, if that's all right."

"Yes, I'd like that," I said. He edged toward me and I met him halfway to kiss him good night. Then I got out, closed the car door softly, and ran into the house. There was just a small lamp on in the hallway. I tiptoed up the stairs. They creaked like tattletales, and when I reached the landing, Mommy stepped to her bedroom doorway.

"Have fun, Honey?" she asked. She was in her nightgown, her hair down around her shoulders.

"Yes."

"Good. Okay, sleep well. We have a big day on the farm tomorrow," she said to explain why they were all asleep already.

Besides our usual chores, there was the planting of the north field, and I knew that Daddy and Grandad had some repair work to do on the grain combine, the machine we used to harvest our corn in the fall.

"Good night, Mommy," I said and entered my room.

My mind was so heavily occupied with all that had happened on my date with Chandler that I didn't see what was on my bed until I actually had gone to the bathroom, put on my nightgown, and reached for the blanket to turn it back and crawl under.

There, prominently before me, was Grandad's old Bible with a faded blue ribbon inserted in the pages to mark a place. For a moment I stood there frozen, almost too afraid to touch it. Grandad had once told me the story of a sinful woman who, when she attended Communion at her church, choked to death on a wafer.

"When a soiled soul confronts something holy, the Lord's retribution is mighty and dreadful," he said.

I thought about calling Mommy to show her what he had done, but I was afraid. What if something terrible happened to her because I made her lift the Bible off my bed? Was I a fool to believe in such things? Despite what I thought of him and his ways,

Grandad Forman was so confident, so sure that he knew what God wanted of us.

To illustrate his confidence, he often pointed to his success as a farmer.

"God rewards me for my devotion," he claimed. "Everything I have, everything I do is dependent upon nature, solidly in the palm of God's very hand. He could wipe me out in an instant," he said, snapping his fingers right before my eyes.

I felt my heart jump in my chest when he did that. As a result of all that, whenever Grandad looked at me, I would think God Himself was looking at me through Grandad's eyes. Sometimes I fled from them, avoided him, afraid that he could actually read my thoughts and know I had dreamed wicked things. All the days of my youth, he seemed to hover over me and around me more than he did anyone else in our family. Why? What did he know about me that I, myself, didn't know? It used to terrify me and still did a little. Was there something dark and evil inside me? Was I what Grandad Forman called, "prime feed for hungry Satan"?

Standing up to him once, Mommy recited Scripture in defiance of his dreadful threats and promises.

"Though I speak with the tongues of men and of angels, and have not charity, I am become as sounding brass, or a tinkling cymbal," she told him, backing him off.

Surely, she was right. Merciful God would not hurt me for anything I had done without knowing why it was sinful, I thought, and I picked up the Bible, intending to put it aside, but I couldn't help being drawn to the pages Grandad obviously had marked for me to read before I went to sleep.

He had marked First Corinthians, 5:11: *But now I have written unto you not to keep company, if any man that is called a brother be a fornicator, or covetous, or an idolater, or a railer or a drunkard, or an extortioner; with such a one, no, not to eat...put away from among yourselves that wicked person.*

What did he mean? Did he mean Chandler? Did he mean me, myself?

How dare he make such an accusation? He had never even met Chandler, how could he condemn us without knowing what was truly in our hearts?

I felt like heaving his Bible and his threats out the window, and actually walked toward it to do just that, but when I started to open the window, I stopped. I couldn't put the blame on the Good Book, and it was sacrilegious to treat it like some garbage. Feeling trapped, I grew furious, went to my desk, and ripped a sheet of paper from my notebook. Using a black Magic Marker so it would be large and prominent, I wrote one of Mommy's favorite retorts: *Judge not that ye be not judged,* and then I taped it to the cover of Grandad's old Bible.

I went to his room and placed it at the foot of his door so it would be the first thing he saw when he rose in the morning. I felt good about it, but I couldn't help trembling. Mommy was the one who stood up to him the best of all of us, certainly not me.

But someday soon I'd like to know why I was his favorite target for his hell and damnation speeches. Why did he see the face of a sinner in me? What had I ever done to give him such thoughts and fears? How could he ever think such dreadfully disgusting thoughts about Uncle Peter and me? It gnawed at my insides like some ache that would never go away. I vowed I would know the answers.

Yet, I was almost as afraid of the answers as I was of the questions themselves.

Saturday was the long and difficult day it had promised to be. By the time I rose and went down to breakfast, Daddy and Grandad were long in the fields with Uncle Simon. I looked at Mommy to see if Grandad had said anything about his Bible and what I had taped onto it. I expected he would rail about my defiance and lack of remorse or something, but Mommy's talk was only about how hard Daddy was going to work and how she wished Grandad would agree to hire another man, at least during planting and especially during harvesting.

"Simon does the work of two, maybe even three ordinary men, but your father hates to see him take on so much and do so much of what is his. Your grandad is a different story. The man feeds off his defiance and stubbornness. It fuels him and gives him the strength and energy of a man half his age. Say what you will about Abraham Forman, you have to give the devil his due," Mommy rattled on.

"I'll get out there and help," I said.

"You shouldn't be out there under this sun. Women and girls your age work like that back from where I came, but they quickly grew old beyond their years. I don't like your hands getting too tough and hard. It will hurt your violin playing, Honey."

I looked up with surprise. She had always admired and encouraged my playing, but she didn't speak of it as anything I would definitely do with my future.

"You really think that's important, Mommy?"

She paused in her work and turned to me, wiping her hands on a dish towel.

"Your father and I have had a talk with Mr. Wengrow. That man thinks a great deal of you and your talent. He did from the start. I have a mother's pride, of course, but he's a musician, a teacher, and he thinks you have what it takes to make a life with your violin. He wants us to let you try out for a school in New York City."

"I know," I said.

"Your father's worried about it, but I'm not."

"How come?" I asked.

She sat at the table and reached for my hand to hold.

"You are not much younger than I was when I set out for America with Aunt Ethel," she said. "We arrived in New York City first, and all the traffic and the people, the tall buildings, hustle and bustle was frightening, but," she said with a small smile on her lips, "exciting, too. I had lived my whole life in a small country village. I thought I had landed on another planet, and don't forget, our English was not so good then, but we had some cousins who helped us and then we came here to Ohio to live.

"You have lived all your life in a rural world, too, but you have had the advantage of being in big cities and seeing what it's really like on television and in your movies. It won't be as strange to you, and you're a good girl, Honey. You'll always do the right thing, I'm sure. I'm not worried," she emphasized. "If it's right for you, you'll be right for it."

"I don't know if I am, Mommy. I don't know if I'm really as good as Mr. Wengrow thinks."

"Well, we'll find out," she said, patting my hand and rising. "What will be will be."

"Daddy agreed then?"

"Daddy agreed," she said. Her smile faded

quickly. "Don't expect any encouragement from your grandfather. He'll be reciting prayers for the dead as soon as you set out."

"Why does he think so little of me, Mommy? Why does he *expect* me to be a sinner?" I asked her.

She shook her head.

"It's his way with everyone," she said and continued her work.

"No, it's not, Mommy. You know it's not. He's always been on me, lecturing, warning, trying to frighten me into being a good girl. Why?" I pursued.

"It's his way," she repeated, this time with her back to me.

I told her what he had done the night before with his Bible and what I had done in return. She listened, her eyes growing smaller and darker.

Then she nodded.

"I thought he was quieter this morning and had that mad gleam in his eyes, like someone who had seen Satan himself stroll through the house."

"I'm afraid of him," I admitted.

She stared at me and nodded again.

"It's good that you'll leave this place," she said with such vehemence, I lost my breath for a moment.

"But why, Mommy? Why do you say it like that?"

"I just do."

"Why is Grandad so stern with me?"

"Because he's a sinner himself," she blurted.

"I don't understand, Mommy. How is he, of all people, a sinner? Because he won't go to church?"

"No."

"Then why, Mommy?"

"Leave it be, Honey. Go on, play your violin. Practice," she ordered and once again turned her back on me.

It left me cold, even colder than I had felt when I had seen Grandad's Bible on my bed.

Chandler phoned mid-afternoon and asked me if he could come by.

"I have something I want to give you," he said.

"What?"

"If I tell you, it won't be a surprise."

I laughed and told him to come. Then I told Mommy. Daddy, Uncle Simon, and Grandad were still out in the fields. I waited outside for Chandler, who arrived even sooner than I had anticipated. He stepped out of his car and handed me a gift-wrapped box.

"What is this? Why did you buy me something? It's not my birthday or anything," I said.

"I don't need a reason to buy you something," he insisted. He looked so intense, so determined, I nodded.

"What is it?" I sat on the front steps and undid the ribbon, then tore away the paper and opened the box. There was a pile of sheet music within, all for the violin.

"Chandler, this is a lot. It must have cost a lot, too," I said, thumbing through the pieces. I estimated well over two hundred dollars worth.

"It's all Bartok," he said. "You've got An Evening in the Village, First and Second Sonata, First Rhapsody, Hungarian folk tunes, and Romanian folk dances. I was thinking about your audition and what you should prepare for it. I suggest the First Sonata and something from the Romanian folk dances. Anyone would get a good view of your ability from that."

"Thank you, Chandler," I said. "It's a wonderful gift and you brought it at the right time. My parents are going to let me try. Mr. Wengrow convinced them."

"I knew he would," Chandler said.

"Well, you knew more than I did." I embraced the box of music and stood up. "Thank you," I repeated and kissed him on the cheek.

Just as I did, Grandad, Daddy, and Uncle Simon came around the barn. My heart stopped and started. Daddy waved, but after a moment's hard stare, Grandad turned and went into the barn, with Uncle Simon trailing behind him.

"Come inside," I said. "I'll put this away and we'll go for a walk."

Chandler said hello to Mommy, who made conversation with him while I put away the gift of music. Then we left the house and I took him toward the pond.

"This is my favorite place here," I said. "I used to spend time with my uncle Peter here."

Chandler nodded, gazing around.

"Very peaceful, pretty."

"Sometimes I sit on the dock and dip my naked feet in the water. Minnows swim around my toes."

"Let's do it," Chandler said, and sat to take off his shoes and socks. I laughed and did the same.

"Wow, that's a lot colder than I expected," he cried when his feet hit the water. "I think my ankles are going to turn blue. How come it's not bothering you?"

"I guess I'm just used to it," I said with a shrug.

"All I've ever been in is a heated pool."

He closed his eyes to endure it, then finally surrendered and brought his feet out, curling his legs so he could rub his ankles. I laughed and helped, rubbing the chill out vigorously.

"You must have steel flowing through your veins to enjoy that," he said.

"Feeling better?"

"Yes, thanks."

"It's refreshing. It wakes you up," I said.

"I was awake, thank you!"

I brought my feet completely out and he rubbed mine, too.

"In some countries, we'd have to get married now," he said. "Touching someone's naked feet is very intimate."

We looked into each other's eyes, locked in the warm flow of our gazes. I knew he wanted to kiss me and I wanted him to kiss me. I spun around and lowered myself to his lap, the move taking him by delightful surprise. He laughed, moved to make me comfortable, and began to stroke my hair.

"You grew up in a very beautiful place, Honey. I'm jealous. I wish I had a place like this to run to when I wanted to be by myself, instead of just closing my bedroom door or putting on my headphones and turning up the music. It's all in you: the water, the fresh smell of wild grass and wildflowers, the sunlight. It gives you your glow, makes you blossom."

"Funny you say that. Uncle Simon thinks of me like he does his precious flowers."

"He's right."

He touched my lips and I kissed the tip of his fingers. He smiled, lowered my head gently from his thigh to the floor of the dock and spread out beside me so we were face to face. Then he kissed the tip of my nose.

"I might come to you someday," he said, "and remind you I've touched your naked feet. Then I might ask you to marry me, Honey."

"I don't know if I'll ever get married."

"Sure you will. If anyone might not, it's me," he said. "I haven't had good examples. My parents aren't exactly poster children for the institution. But," he continued, running his finger down the side of my face and under my chin, "with you, I'm sure it would be very different. You're real.

"Although," he added, "sometimes I think you're too good to be true and you really are just a dream. The only way I'm sure is when I do this," he said, and leaned forward to kiss me.

I closed my eyes. I felt the warm breeze and smelled the fresh water and the scent of wildflowers. I breathed deeply, filling myself with such happiness and pleasure as his lips lingered on mine, and then I opened my eyes and gasped.

Grandad was standing over us, gazing down, his eyes blazing, a machete in his hand.

For a second Chandler didn't realize Grandad was there and looked confused by my expression. Then he turned on his back, looked up at Grandad, and practically leaped to his feet in a single move.

"Sinners," Grandad accused, waving the machete at Chandler. "And on my land. You'll turn it into Sodom and Gomorrah, just as I was told you would," he fired at me. His eyes widened. "The prophecies, the prophecies!"

"We didn't do anything wrong, Mr. Forman," Chandler began to protest. "We were just..."

"Fornicator. Get thee away, Satan," Grandad ordered, raising the machete again. Chandler's eyes nearly popped. He backed up, looking confused and frightened. I got to my feet and scooped up our shoes and socks. I took his arm and marched him off the dock.

"Don't look back at him. Just keep walking," I said.

"He's crazy. Wow! He was going to kill me, I think. Would he swing that at me, really? Is he coming after us?"

"Just keep walking," I muttered, the tears choking my throat.

Grandad was shouting biblical phrases at us.

"I'm sorry, Chandler. I didn't think he would come sneaking around after us. I thought they were working on the grain combine."

"What's wrong with him?"

"He's afraid of going to hell," I said, gazing back. He looked like a mad prophet raging against the heavens, his arms lifted, that machete pointed in our direction.

"He should be locked up somewhere. He's dangerous."

Daddy and Uncle Simon had just parted and Daddy was stepping onto the porch when we appeared, hurrying from the path to the pond toward Chandler's car. Both he and Uncle Simon turned to watch us a moment.

"Why are you guys walking barefoot? Something wrong, Honey?" Daddy asked when we drew closer.

"Grandad," I said.

"What did he do?"

"He frightened us and accused us of things," I said. "And he waved his machete at Chandler."

"He did what?"

Daddy and Uncle Simon looked toward the pond.

"I'd better get going," Chandler said, reaching for his car door handle. He didn't pause to put on his shoes and socks first. "I'll call you. Or, maybe you call me when you can," he added. He looked absolutely terrified. I couldn't blame him.

"I'm sorry," I said. He nodded, started the engine, and drove off quickly, forgetting the bump again.

I looked up at Daddy.

"He's horrible," I cried. "I don't care if he is your father and my grandfather. He's just horrible. I hate him!" I shouted and ran up the steps, past Daddy and into the house, not looking back.

Inside, I burst into tears.

"Honey!" Mommy shouted after me as I charged up the stairs. "Why are you barefoot? What's wrong?"

"Grandad!" I cried. "I wish he was dead!"

Such was the mad old man's influence and effect on me all my life that I immediately regretted saying such a thing. I bit down on my lip so hard, I could taste the blood. If God was nearby, waiting to swoop down on me for being an evil person, He would surely do so now, I thought.

Shivering and wishing I could crawl inside myself and hide, I threw myself on my bed, embraced myself, and closed my eyes, waiting for the sound of thunder even on a day like this.

All that followed was silence and the slow ticking down of my racing heart until I drifted into a welcome sleep.

10

—⁓—

Sins of the Father

When I awoke, I was greeted with a funereal silence. Mommy had let me sleep and it was well into the early evening. Through my window I could see the last vestiges of daylight were clinging to the horizon like the hands of a drowning person hoping to be pulled back up. The yellow shafts of thin light against the inky sky resembled fingers, reaching, searching for help.

I sat up, scrubbed my face with my dry hands and sighed so deeply, I thought I would crack my spine. I listened again for any sounds, but I didn't even hear the drone of the television set or anyone's footsteps or muffled voice. For an additional few moments I sat there, resurrecting the terrible moments at the pond. I saw Chandler's expression of terror and shock again and again. Surely, he would not want to have a thing to do with me now. He must believe I came from madness.

I rose and went downstairs slowly, still listening for someone. I found Mommy sitting on the front porch in her rocking chair. She had a knitted shawl wrapped around herself and her eyes were closed.

"Mommy?" I said, and she sat up.

"How are you, Honey? Hungry?"

"No. What's going on? Where's Daddy and Grandad?"

"Daddy and Grandad had a very bad argument after what happened," she began. "I thought they would come to blows. Actually, I thought Grandad would swing that machete at him. Your uncle Simon stepped between them and just stood there like a wall, and they stopped.

"It calmed down. They ate some dinner and then went out to work on the grain combine. That's where the two of them are. Simon went up to his room. He's got a bad cold, probably from having only cold water to bathe in and sleeping in that dank, dark place."

"Did he get his dinner?"

"I brought it to him," she said. "Why don't you have something to eat now, Honey?"

"I was so embarrassed, Mommy," I moaned.

"Chandler will probably have nothing to do with me now."

"Oh, I'm sure he will," she said.

"You weren't there. It was terrible. I was never so frightened myself."

"I know. Let me make you something to eat," she insisted, rising. "At least some hot soup."

She put her arm around me and we went inside.

After I ate a little, I picked up my violin and began to play. More and more lately, I was finding it helped me express my innermost feelings. The music always revealed what was truly going on within the caverns of my heart. I didn't play that long, but when I gazed out my window, I saw Uncle Simon had been sitting by his, listening. He had a light on, and he looked different because his head was slumped. I supposed he had fallen asleep. I waited to see if he would wake and wave good night, but he didn't, so I put away my violin.

I was feeling very, very tired myself. The emotional drain was deeper than I had imagined. Maybe I was just very depressed, but almost before I let my head fall back on the pillow, my eyes closed, and the next thing I knew, the light of morning was brightening my room.

The house was quiet. When I glanced at my clock, I saw it was well after nine. We usually left for church between eight and eight-thirty. I rose, washed, and dressed as quickly as I could. When I descended the stairs, I found Mommy had left a note for me on the refrigerator door.

Daddy and I decided to let you sleep this morning. There's pancake batter in a bowl in the refrigerator. Eat a good breakfast. We'll see you after church.

I wondered where Grandad was. I was certainly not in the mood for any of his hell and damnation speeches and had made up my mind that if he started on me and Chandler, I would either walk away or tell him to mind his own business. My indignation fueled my courage and fired up my anger. I marched around the kitchen, slamming pans and silverware harder than necessary. I needed noise. The silence made it feel as if the world was closing in on me.

I ate deliberately, chewing hard, swallowing and digging my fork into my pancakes as if I had to kill each one before I could eat it. All the while I had my eyes fixed on that doorway, anticipating my grandad's entrance, but he did not come. Winding down, I finished eating and washed and put away my dishes, the pancake skillet, and silverware. By the time everything was cleared away and cleaned, I heard Daddy's truck pull up in front of the house. I stepped out to greet them.

"Morning, Honey," Daddy called.

"Did you make yourself some breakfast, dear?" Mommy asked immediately.

"Yes," I said. "Sorry I slept so late."

"That's all right. We were glad you got whatever rest you needed, dear," Mommy said.

She looked very pretty and fresh this morning, and I thought Daddy was very handsome in his sports jacket, tie, and slacks. Mommy paused to kiss me on the forehead. Then her eyes got small and dark.

"He bother you any this morning?"

"I haven't seen or heard him."

"Grandad's up in the west field, probably," Daddy said. "There's a wooded place there he's used on Sunday as his private church for years."

I knew the place. Because Grandad Forman put such a holy stamp on it and because it was his private place, I stayed away from it.

"He's been troubling," Mommy told Daddy. "And I don't mean just the incident yesterday with Honey and Chandler, Isaac. There's a new madness in him. When he came at you yesterday, I thought he would swing that machete for sure," Mommy said. "He's mumbling to himself and talking to the shadows more than ever. It's not good."

Daddy nodded and gazed toward the west field.

"I know," he said. "He and I worked together as usual afterward, but he would barely speak to me and kept reciting phrases from the Bible. It gave me the creeps the way he turned his head when he spoke, as if some invisible person was there beside him."

"It's troublesome. Very troublesome, Isaac," Mommy emphasized.

"I'll try to talk to him some more and get him calmed down," Daddy promised. "He should be back soon."

"I haven't seen Uncle Simon this morning either," I said.

"Oh, Simon's still quite under the weather today, Honey. He's been developing a bad chest cold and I told him to make sure he rests himself well," Daddy said.

"Did he have his breakfast?"

"I brought him some hot oatmeal before we left for church," Mommy said. "Well, I guess I'll go change into something more ordinary."

"Me, too," Daddy said.

I looked at the barn. It was so rare for Uncle Simon to be under the weather and incapacitated. I thought he was invincible. If he was sick enough to stay in his claustrophobic room, it had to be serious.

"Maybe Uncle Simon should see a doctor and have some medicine," I said.

"You know how he is about that," Mommy replied. "I'll make him some chicken soup for lunch."

She and Daddy went inside. I stood there thinking

awhile and then I went in and fetched my violin and the box of music Chandler had bought for me.

"I'm going over to see Uncle Simon," I shouted to Mommy and Daddy, who were still changing clothes.

I went to the barn and then up the stairway to Uncle Simon's room. He didn't reply when I knocked on his door, so I opened it and peered in. He was in bed. I thought he was asleep, but as soon as I started to back out and close the door, his eyes opened.

"Honey," he said, followed with a flow of coughs. "Something the matter?"

"No, Uncle Simon. I was just coming over to practice my violin and see if you needed anything."

"Oh," he said. He wiped strands of hair off his forehead and propped himself up. He wasn't wearing any shirt, and there was a patch of redness at the center of his chest.

"Do you have a fever?" I asked him.

"No," he said, shaking his head vigorously. He coughed again.

"That doesn't sound good, Uncle Simon."

"It's nothing," he insisted.

"Mommy's making you some chicken soup, but if you don't feel better soon, you should go to a doctor," I said firmly.

He nodded, but with no real conviction.

"You're going to play the violin for me?" he asked, finally showing some light and excitement in his eyes.

"I wanted to start on some of the music my friend Chandler Maxwell gave me yesterday. I'm going to audition for a special school in New York City," I explained.

His eyes widened with amazement.

"New York City?"

"Uh-huh."

I took my violin out of its case and pulled one of his two chairs up closer to the bed. Then I sat, opened the box of music, and sifted through the sheets, deciding to start with Bartok's First Sonata.

"I'm just learning this," I explained.

He nodded, looking fascinated. It warmed my heart to see how I was cheering him up and helping him feel better already. He propped himself up a little more and waited. I tuned up and warmed up and then I started on the music. Every time I stopped to start again, he nodded enthusiastically.

"I really shouldn't do this without Mr. Wengrow. It's hard judging yourself."

I started again and I played for quite a while before stopping. When I glanced at him, I saw that he had closed his eyes. The music appeared to have soothed him, but his face was very flushed. I set the violin down, and he looked at me with some surprise.

"You look like you've got a high fever, Uncle Simon," I said.

I went to him and put my lips to his forehead. It was the way Mommy always tested for a fever.

I had barely done so when Grandad's cry made me jump and turn quickly toward the doorway where he stood, clutching his Bible. I hadn't heard him come up the stairs.

"Jezebel!" he screamed. "Get away from him."

"He's sick, Grandad."

Grandad nodded and smiled so coldly it sent a chill across the room and into my heart.

"Yes, he's sick," he said. "Sick with the strain of evil that's in you both. You'll bring down the Lord's vengeance on me! Whore!" he cried.

Tears flowed so quickly and freely from my eyes, I couldn't flick them away fast enough.

Suddenly Uncle Simon rose from his bed, and to my shock, he was naked. He waved his mallet of a fist at Grandad.

"Get out of here with your garbage talk," he roared. It felt like a crash of thunder.

Grandad stared wide-eyed, as if he was looking at the Angel of Death. He pointed at him.

"Sinner!" he shouted, turned, and fled.

Uncle Simon quickly realized he was uncovered and seized the blanket to wrap around himself.

"You better go," he said.

My heart was pounding a hole through my chest and back. I shivered and trembled, gathering my music, putting my violin back into its case.

"I'll tell Mommy what happened," I promised. "You didn't do anything wrong."

Uncle Simon was back under the blanket, his eyes shut, his thumb and fingers pressing on his temples.

"You need a doctor," I insisted and hurried out, never so frightened. I checked the yard for signs of Grandad and then rushed to the house.

Mommy was in the kitchen working on her chicken soup when I burst in. For a moment, I couldn't speak. She looked at me, saw how upset I was, and dropped the knife she was using to cut up a carrot. It clattered on the floor.

"What's wrong?"

"Grandad...Uncle Simon," I blurted. "It was a terrible scene!"

Daddy heard the commotion and hurried down the stairs.

"What happened?"

As quickly as I could get out the words, I described what had occurred, how just as I had innocently checked on Uncle Simon's temperature, Grandad appeared in the doorway and called me names. Without saying Uncle Simon was naked, I told how he had jumped up and threatened to bash Grandad with his fist. I spoke so quickly, it turned my throat into a tunnel with sandpaper walls. Mommy had to give me a glass of water to finish

"Isaac," Mommy said. "It's come to pass. I feel it. I know it."

"I'll get out there," he said. He went for his boots.

"Be careful," she cried after him.

"What's come to pass?" I asked.

Mommy shook her head and sat hard on a chair, lowering her forehead to her propped hand.

"Mommy?"

She shook her head and sighed. Just as she lifted it to speak, we heard the most ghastly, animal scream. The look in Mommy's face matched my own terror.

"Isaac," she cried and the two of us ran out of the house.

The shouting was coming from the area behind the barn where Uncle Simon had his wonderful garden. Mommy reached for my hand as the two of us ran across the yard. When we turned the corner of the barn, we saw Uncle Simon. He was barefoot, wearing only jeans and holding a scythe in the air, poised to bring it down on Grandad, who was sprawled on the ground.

Flowers everywhere had been slashed with that scythe. The garden was decimated. Daddy was on the sidelines, his hand extended toward Uncle Simon, who stood like a pillar of rage over my grandfather.

"Don't do it, Simon," Daddy pleaded. "You can't do it."

Uncle Simon's arms shook with the effort to hold back and the effort to sweep down. There was no doubt in my mind that he had the power to slice Grandad in half.

"Simon!" Mommy shouted. She let go of my hand. "Isaac, tell him. Tell him!" she commanded Daddy. He looked at her, then at me, and then he stepped closer.

"Simon, he's your father," he said. "He's your real father."

Uncle Simon looked at Daddy and then down at Grandad, who had his arm extended up to try to ward off the deadly blow when it came. He clutched his Bible in his hand as if it would act as a shield.

Uncle Simon shook his head.

"Yes," Daddy said. "It's true, Simon. It's true. Tell him!" he shouted at Grandad.

To me it seemed as if the air had stopped moving around us and we were frozen in time. Nothing moved, not a bird, not a rabbit. The whole world was holding its breath.

Grandad shook his head.

"I don't confess to him," he cried. "I don't confess to him."

"Simon," Mommy said in a softer tone. "Isaac is

telling you the truth. You can't do this. We'll make it all right. Please, Simon."

I was crying and shaking so much, I couldn't have spoken if I had wanted to. Uncle Simon gazed down at Grandad a moment and then he tossed away the scythe and marched toward his flowers, kneeling down to repair whatever he could.

Grandad Forman rose slowly. He looked from Daddy to Mommy to me and shook his head, backing away. He pointed at me.

"It's in the blood," he said. "My sins are carried in the blood."

"No!" Mommy shouted back at him. "Your sins were born and will die with you, not with us. Go make your own peace and leave us be," she ordered.

He turned and stumbled away, clutching his chest with one hand, his Bible with the other. After a few steps, he paused to look back at us. He was mumbling to himself and looked insane, his hair flying up every which way.

"Go into the house, Dad," Daddy shouted at him.

Grandad shook his head and then walked faster, almost running toward the west field as if he had to flee. We saw him stumble and fall and then get up and hurry along, gazing back at us until he was nearly gone from sight.

"I'd better go after him," Daddy said.

"Leave him, Isaac. We've got to get Simon to

bed," Mommy said, stepping toward him. She put her hand on Uncle Simon's shoulder. "Go back to bed, Simon. You need rest before you get very, very sick. Isaac and Honey will repair what can be repaired for you."

"She's right, Simon," Daddy said. "Go on back to bed."

Simon stared at his mutilated garden, two large tears flowing from his eyes.

"I'll fix whatever can be fixed, Uncle Simon," I promised, tears falling from my chin as well.

"You'll plant again, Simon," Mommy said. "Go on."

Daddy put his hand under Uncle Simon's arm, more to urge him up than to lift him. He rose, slowly, looking after Grandad, not so much with hate and anger in his face now as much as confusion.

"I won't let him be my father," he said.

Mommy smiled.

"I don't blame you," she said.

Uncle Simon shook his head. He looked at the destroyed garden and then toward the direction Grandad had fled.

"Can't be," he said. "Can't be."

He let Daddy guide him away.

"Wait," Mommy called after them. Daddy turned to her. "Don't take him back to that barn. Take him to Peter's room in the house," she ordered.

Daddy smiled and nodded.

"C'mon, Simon. It's time you came home," Daddy told him.

Mommy put her arm around me. I had finally stopped shaking and had swallowed down the lump that had closed my throat. My tears felt frozen over my eyes.

"You all right, Honey?"

"Yes." I looked over the devastated garden. "I'll fix whatever I can."

"Okay. I'll go finish making the soup and give him something for his fever." She looked after Grandad Forman. "If that lunatic comes back, come into the house to tell me."

"You weren't telling the truth, Mommy, were you? You made that up about Grandad being Uncle Simon's real father just so he wouldn't hurt him, right?"

"No, Honey, it *is* the truth. Your grandmother Jennie told your father about it years ago. Her sister Tessie and her first husband worked for Grandad, and Grandad committed a sinful act with her. She became pregnant, and soon after, her husband was killed. He died never knowing, which was a good thing, I suppose. Grandad then married Tess, but Simon was a living reminder of his sin, so he treated him badly and eventually, after Jennie's death, tried to keep him out of his mind by moving him out of the house.

"After Jennie died, the sin was a heavier weight on

his conscience, I suppose. He believed God was punishing him again by taking her. He became even more crazed with his biblical visions.

"Her sister Jennie didn't want to marry him, but he forced her to by describing Tess as a seductress and making Jennie feel a responsibility to Simon. She was a good woman and she cared lovingly for Simon, Peter, and your father, but that didn't stop Grandad from seeing his demons in all of us."

"And so Grandad thought I would be a sinner because he had been? That's why he's always been all over me with his threats of hell and damnation?"

"Yes, but you must not let any of that affect you, Honey. It's his private madness and his own guilt that makes him think most of the crazy things he declares and does.

"For a long time, your daddy felt sorry for him. He tried always to be a dutiful son, to help him live with himself, to recover. He was too good a son, if you ask me."

"Did Uncle Peter know all this, too?"

"Not according to your father, no. Your grandmother never told him. He was different—a lighter spirit—and she didn't want to put any burden on him that would change him. He was her favorite, but Daddy didn't mind that. In a way, they were both protecting Peter."

"Poor Uncle Simon, though. Why was he tortured for his father's sins, left in the dark alone?"

Mommy smiled.

"I've always felt he was better off living without the knowledge and being estranged from your grandfather. In his way, I think Simon has found some contentment," she added, looking at the broken flowers.

"And now Grandad has even destroyed that," I said mournfully.

"It will be repaired, and if I know Simon, it will be better and bigger. Daddy is definitely going ahead with that greenhouse idea, too."

"Good."

"I better get inside and help with Simon. I'm sorry all this came out this way, Honey, but I never doubted that some day it would. It festered on your grandfather's soul and leaked poison into his heart for a long time. Maybe he can find some peace now as well."

I nodded.

"Don't ever think something is wrong with you or you have a strain of evil in you because of him. His sins live and die with him," Mommy assured me.

She kissed me, squeezed me to her, and then walked toward the house.

I turned to what looked like a battlefield and began to repair what little could be restored.

Maybe it was the effect of being in Uncle Peter's room. Uncle Simon had loved him so much. Or maybe it was Mommy's wonderful homemade soup.

Maybe it was a good dose of aspirin, or maybe it was a combination of everything, but Uncle Simon relaxed, his face looked far less flushed, and he fell into a comfortable sleep very soon afterward.

"We'll move him back into the house permanently," Daddy vowed.

"I think if he still has a high fever, we should take him to see Dr. Spalding tomorrow," Mommy said.

"I'll try," Daddy told her. "He might not want to be blood-related to Dad, but he shares some of his stubbornness. That's for sure."

Mommy laughed.

Could we find a way to mend all this? I wondered. How I loved the both of them for their eternal optimism, for the way they bore down and gritted their teeth no matter what difficulties arose. I hoped and prayed I had their perseverance. I knew if I intended to go forward with a career in music and entertainment, I would surely need it. Rejection and defeats would be all over the road to any sort of success.

The day went on. I kept hoping to hear from Chandler, but he didn't call, and I wasn't up to calling him just yet. I had worked in the garden for nearly an hour, fixing what I could, and then I came in, showered, and joined Mommy and Daddy in the kitchen, where they were just getting ready to have a late lunch.

"It's been hours, Isaac," she told him. "I guess you'll have to see what's become of him."

Daddy nodded.

"Should I come with you, Daddy?" I asked him.

"No, it's not necessary," he said.

"Maybe she should, Isaac," Mommy said. The worry in his eyes made him reconsider.

"Okay, sure," he said. "He's probably still up in the west field."

"Hopefully, coming to his senses," Mommy said.

Daddy nodded, and he and I left.

"Was it true that Uncle Peter never knew any of this, Daddy?" I asked as we walked over the field.

"Sometimes I felt he did, that he knew instinctively. He never asked any questions or made any statements, and I never brought it up with him. Peter was Grandad's only window on happiness and light. I couldn't find it in my heart to close that window. You remember how Grandad would chastise him but do it relatively gently. I never saw him take a strap to him or ever strike him.

"I suppose Peter was some sort of salvation, some sort of redemption to him."

"But Daddy, Grandad accused me of doing sordid things with Uncle Peter."

"Only after Peter's death. Whatever hope or strain of kindness lingered in my father died with Peter that day, and of course, Grandad assumed it was God's way of imposing additional punishment. He blamed himself. He blamed you. He blamed us all. It's as though he believes we're all infected with the disease of his own sins.

"I know you hate him for what he did to Uncle Simon's garden and the things he's been saying to you, but you don't hate him half as much as he hates himself, Honey. Just remember that if you can, and maybe you can find some part of yourself that will forgive him and sympathize. It will make you feel better, believe me," Daddy said.

I nodded, my eyes filling as I realized, perhaps for the first time, how wise and kind he really was.

"I will, Daddy," I promised. "I will."

"I know you will, Honey. The one thing Grandad's failed to realize is you are his salvation. You are his redemption. You're the promise every rainbow leaves behind for us."

He embraced me and we walked like that until we saw the patch of forest ahead of us.

"I don't see him there," Daddy said, shading his eyes with his right hand.

I didn't either.

"Maybe he went home a different way, or maybe he went somewhere else."

"Maybe," he said, but his eyes continued to be narrow and suspicious as we continued toward the woods.

We were only about a hundred yards from it when Daddy stopped and seized my hand.

"What?" I asked and gazed ahead. Slowly, I could discern Grandad sprawled on his back.

"I see him. He's asleep. Let's not frighten him," Daddy said. We walked slowly, quietly.

"Dad," my daddy called softly. He raised his voice and called again.

Grandad Forman did not respond. I could see he had his Bible on his chest and both his hands over it.

"Dad!"

Daddy hurried into the patch of woods. I lingered a dozen feet back and watched as Daddy knelt down beside Grandad and shook him. Then he put his fingers on Grandad's neck and searched for a pulse. After a moment he lowered his head.

"Daddy?"

He lifted his head and looked at me.

"What's wrong with him?"

Daddy shook his head.

"Go back to the house, Honey, and tell Mommy your grandad's gone. He's found his peace."

11

~m~

Heart Song

Grandad Forman's funeral wasn't a big one. Most of the friends and acquaintances he had were either dead or too sick and weak to attend. Chandler's father attended, and Chandler accompanied him. His mother didn't. There were a few other business people there and some friends of Daddy's and Mommy's. I didn't think Uncle Simon would want to go, but he surprised me.

He also surprised Mommy and Daddy by agreeing to go see a doctor. Dr. Spalding put him on an antibiotic that had an almost immediate effect. His fever diminished and, although his cough lingered, it was far less severe, so he would have no problem attending the services. He had only one set of nice clothes.

Mommy pressed his jacket and pants and Daddy found him a black tie to wear and tied it for him. Mommy even shined and polished Uncle Simon's one and only pair of dress shoes.

It was a simple church service, but it was Daddy's idea that I add to it by playing my violin. As I played, I tried to remember only the good things about Grandad: the pride he took in his work and the success of the farm, his physical strength at his age, and the rare but precious moments when he looked softer, gazing almost lovingly at me.

I saw how proud and happy it made Mommy as I played, and when I looked at Chandler, I saw a glow in his face that warmed my cold, dark heart. I smiled inside and eagerly greeted him at the end of the service.

"I'm sorry I haven't called you," he told me. "I thought first that I might have had something to do with all this."

"You didn't and neither did I, Chandler."

"When are you coming back to school?"

"Tomorrow," I said, and then hurried to join Mommy, Daddy, and Uncle Simon for our trip to the cemetery. Grandad's first wife Tess was buried beside her first husband. Grandad was to be laid beside my grandmother Jennie.

"I'm not so sure she's happy about that," Mommy whispered.

We smiled secretly through our eyes, and we held

hands while the final words were spoken over the coffin and Grandad was lowered into the earth from which he had made his living and did love. No one was more willing to become dust unto dust, I thought.

I joined Uncle Simon, who had gone to visit his mother's grave. He was just standing there, staring at the tombstone as if he could see her face in the granite. I knew that from time to time Daddy drove him here to plant flowers.

"She died before I could hear her speak. I don't remember her at all," he said mournfully.

"She's inside you, Uncle Simon. You carry her in your heart."

He nodded and took my hand. We stood there for a moment longer and then joined the others.

The four of us drove back to the farm in relative silence, all of us reliving our own memories and dealing in our own way with the reality that death to someone close to us brings.

I was so happy to return to school the following day. I couldn't get enough homework or be bored in any class. I bathed in the noise and the chatter in the hallways and cafeteria. I even welcomed the envy and green eyes of some of my classmates when they saw how closely Chandler and I kept to each other. Anyone could see there was something special going on by the way our eyes lingered on each other's faces.

My lessons with Mr. Wengrow became more intense. He was very pleased with the music Chandler had bought for me and agreed with the choices for my audition. I practiced obsessively. I looked forward to our joint lessons and I saw how Chandler made Mr. Wengrow concentrate far more on me than on him.

Almost nightly now I would play for Uncle Simon, Mommy, and Daddy in the living room. The music that had once been kept closed in to avoid Grandad's criticism and dire predictions of evil was set free, flowing through the house and over the grounds. As the weather improved and evenings became warmer, I would play outside at night. I would even bring my violin along and play while Daddy and Uncle Simon worked in the fields sometimes. My instrument and I were inseparable. Extra help was hired and they all looked at me and listened with amazement, hearing this kind of music while they worked.

"I wouldn't be surprised if she's sleeping with that violin beside her," Daddy kidded.

"It's not too far from me at any time," I said.

Chandler and I went out both Friday and Saturday nights now, and there were weekends when he visited with us and watched television and then took walks with me. We sat at the pond often. He claimed the water was warming and he could stand dipping his feet in as long as I could.

One night in late May, a particularly warm one, we decided to go swimming. It was an impulsive and exciting decision, because we were going to skinny-dip. I brought out two large towels for us, and under a moonless sky with many stars throwing down a silvery rain of light, we undressed with our backs to each other and then waded in and dove down, crying out in both pleasure and shock. We embraced and kissed, feeling our naked bodies touch in the water. He kissed my breasts and held me as we listened to the symphony around us: the peepers, the frogs, an owl inserting its inquisitive "Who? Who? Who?"

Afterward, wrapped in the towels, we held each other and kissed again. We came the closest to doing the most intimate act of love. Despite burying my childhood fears and driving the demons from our lives after Grandad's passing, I couldn't stop imagining his face glowing in the darkness, his eyes like the tips of candlelight, watching us.

I buried my face in Chandler's chest and made him stop. He held me tightly.

"Not yet," I said. "Not here."

"Okay. I love you, though, Honey. I don't want to do this with anyone else."

"Me neither," I admitted.

I knew that it would be wonderful, but I couldn't help being afraid that, once we did it, once the mystery and the longing was gone, we might lose interest in each other. Chandler continually promised that would never be, but I was afraid of promises. The sun always promised the flowers it would be there for them, but gray days came and so did long, hard rains, washing away the soil. A promise is just a hope, I thought, and a hope is a plan, a dream for the future. It needs much more to make it work, to make it grow. It needs the same tender loving care Uncle Simon gave his seedlings and his plants.

Were we ready to make such a commitment to each other? I wondered. *What would happen to us once we were separated by great distance?*

It made me hesitate, and hope that my hesitation wouldn't discourage Chandler too much and give him doubts about my love for him and his own love for me. Meanwhile, the music continued to bind us, to weave itself around and through us, sewing us together in ways other people couldn't even imagine. Sometimes, I had the feeling we were making love through our music, touching each other very intimately. Mr. Wengrow seemed to feel it, too, and often looked embarrassed by just being there between us, near us.

"I've given you both all that I have," he finally decided. "It's time for you to go out and grow with people far more equipped than I am."

He learned that there was just one more opening at the Senetsky School, and I would be competing with three other prime candidates for it. I was scheduled to audition early in the afternoon on the first Saturday in June. Daddy and Mommy were going to fly to New York with me the day before. I thought it would be a very expensive gamble, and then I wondered how we would pay for my tuition if I should be fortunate enough to be selected. Daddy surprised me with a revelation.

"Your grandad was truly one of the most successful farmers in Ohio, Honey. He wasn't exactly a miser, but he was pretty frugal, as you know. He didn't live or run this farm as if it was successful. He ran everything as if we were on the verge of bankruptcy.

"The truth is, I never knew exactly how much money he had, we had. He liked keeping me in the dark about it, I guess. After the funeral, we met with Mr. Ruderman, Grandad's accountant, and learned about the trust funds.

"The truth is," Daddy said, flashing a smile at Mommy, who was smiling already, "we're probably richer than your boyfriend's family. So don't worry about the money. Worry about the music!"

I did as he suggested, honing my skill with the violin. Getting into this school, winning approval from someone outside of my circle of family and friends had become paramount. It would truly give me the wings I needed to fly off and become whatever I was capable of becoming. The adventure, the risk, all the excitement filled my days and nights with tons of impatience.

Finally, the day came. We were packed and ready to drive to the airport. Just before we left, I went over to say good-bye to Uncle Simon. He was organizing his new flower beds, planning his nursery.

"We're ready to go," I announced. "I'm so nervous, I can barely walk."

He looked at me, and then he bent down and picked up what looked at first like just an ordinary washcloth.

"This is for you," he said, and I carefully opened the fold to see a tiny white carnation.

"It's a flower famous for bringing good luck," he said.

Uncle Simon knew all the symbolism for all his flowers. How Grandad could have ever believed him to be ignorant was beyond my understanding. It was what he had expected because of the sin, I thought, but how unfair and how untrue.

"Thank you, Uncle Simon. I'll keep it close to me," I said. "I'll press it between the pages of my music."

He smiled and I stood on my toes to kiss him good-bye.

He seized my hand unexpectedly as I turned to leave. I looked back at him.

"When you make your music," he said, "think of my flowers. Think you're playing for them."

"I will. Oh, I will, Uncle Simon. Forever."

I ran to join Mommy and Daddy and soon after we drove to the airport.

All three of us were like children entering a toy store when we landed in New York and were driven into the city. It was dark by then and the lights were overwhelming. It was one thing to see it in movies and on television, but a far different and deeper experience to actually be there, to be gazing up at skyscrapers, to see the bridges lit, to hear and see the traffic and the endless stream of people.

Our hotel suite was comfortable—and high enough up to give us a breathtaking view of Manhattan. We were all too excited to fall asleep and watched television almost until midnight. My appointment at the theater in which I was to audition wasn't until eleven. Daddy had planned it out so we would fly back on an early afternoon flight. I trembled, wondering if we would fly back with hope or defeat in our eyes.

We had breakfast and then the hotel doorman called us a taxi. None of us said very much. We sat and looked out the taxi windows, gaping at everything. Actually, I was looking through everything, not really seeing the people and the stores anymore. I was too nervous and afraid. My heart was pounding so hard, I was sure I wouldn't have the strength to lift the violin into position.

Mommy squeezed my hand and smiled confidence into me.

"You'll do your best, Honey," she said. "That's all you can do. After that, whatever is to be will be. When I came here as a young woman, I had to have faith in destiny. I had to believe that what was going to be was good. After you do all you can, there is nothing left but to watch and wait and accept. You must learn how to accept."

"To bend and not break," I repeated. It was one of Daddy's old sayings.

She nodded.

"Exactly."

We arrived at the theater and entered with almost as much curiosity as trepidation. It was an empty theater. There was no one in the lobby to greet us. For a few moments, we stood around. Daddy checked his watch.

"They did say eleven, right?"

"It's on this letter," Mommy emphasized, holding it up. He had read it a number of times anyway.

Suddenly a door to our right burst open and a tall, thin, dark-haired woman emerged, her heels clicking on the tile floor of the small lobby.

"Hello," she said. "You're Honey Forman, I assume?" she asked, holding a paper in her right hand.

She had large brown eyes and a sharp nose. Her lips were pencil-thin and curled a bit up in the corners after she spoke.

"Yes," I said.

"We're running a little late. Just proceed to the stage. There is a music stand on it for you. Start your pieces as quickly as possible," she added.

"I'm Honey's mother and this is her father," Mommy said pointedly.

The tall woman widened her eyes and nodded.

"Yes," she said. "I'm Laura Fairchild, Madam Senetsky's personal assistant. Please," she added, moving to the door. She looked and acted more nervous than I was.

Mommy looked at me, shrugged as if the woman was beyond help, which brought a smile to my lips, and then nodded for us to go forward.

The theater was pitch dark except for the wide spotlight on the stage, which bathed the music stand in light. When our eyes got used to the dark seats, I could make out someone sitting in the rear. It was a woman with her hair pinned up, wearing something very dark and sitting so still, I wondered if she was real or a manikin.

Laura Fairchild gestured toward the stage.

"Please," she said. "We must get started."

Daddy and Mommy took seats and I hurried to the stage. I opened my case and took out my violin and my music. First, I set the music on the stand. My hands were trembling so badly a sheet fell, and I watched it float to the stage floor. I knew I looked amateurish and awkward scooping it up and placing it on the stand, but I couldn't help it. When I placed it there, I saw it had been the sheet over Uncle Simon's little white carnation. The sight of it had an amazing, calming effect on me. I felt myself relax, grow more confident.

After my warm-up, I took a deep breath, remembered all that Mr. Wengrow had emphasized about my posture and demeanor, and began. It was a slow start for me. I wasn't into it as well as I knew I could be. The setting, the rush-rush had chilled my enthusiasm. But suddenly, when I looked out at that dark theater, I envisioned Uncle Simon's flowers. The front row was filled with babies breath, birds of paradise sat beside pink and white carnations. Daisies looked over the heads of forget-me-nots, and on the aisles were blue, yellow, purple, and white irises. Jasmine was scattered throughout.

I could feel the smile spread over my face and fill my heart with joy. I played on, soon flowing into my music, feeling myself soar with the melody.

When I was finished, I couldn't believe how exhausted I felt. The effort had drained me of all my energy, it seemed. For a moment, I couldn't breathe.

"Thank you," I heard Laura Fairchild shout.

Immediately after that, I heard the doors to the theater open and close. Daddy was down at the foot of the stage to help me.

"That was wonderful, Honey," he said. "I never heard you play better."

"If she doesn't want you, she's a fool," Mommy declared before I could say a word of self-criticism.

I laughed to myself. How lucky I was to have parents like these, I thought.

Mommy was angry about the way we were treated. She complained almost all the way home, bringing it up repeatedly.

"Why couldn't the woman introduce herself properly? Why couldn't someone say something encouraging or even something discouraging, for that matter? What sort of a school is this anyway? I want to speak to Mr. Wengrow first chance I get," she said.

"Don't blame him for anything. He was only trying to help her," Daddy cautioned.

Mommy pressed her lips together and shook her head.

"New Yorkers," she muttered. "How rude. Maybe you shouldn't think of it anyway."

I understood she was simply trying to prepare me for a great disappointment. It was loving concern, like putting a bandage on before you even hurt yourself, but I didn't want to be one of those people who turned bitter and turned on their own dreams. I wouldn't be like the famous fox in the fox and the grapes fable, the one who couldn't reach the grapes and so declared them sour anyway.

There was nothing sour about having an opportunity in New York City. I would always dream of it, even if it was beyond my reach.

The days seem to fall away quickly until graduation. All of my fellow students, including the ones who put on the biggest faces of bravado, bragging how far they were getting away from this "dull and boring place," suddenly started to look more like soldiers about to enter battle. Now their faces were full of anxiety, trepidation, and worry. The jokes, the songs, the pounding of the breast and defiance drifted out of our conversations.

The great clock was ticking. It would soon bong the hour when we would be cut away from the big boats that had protected and carried us so far. We would be out there, drifting on our own, making our own course, and either crashing on the rocks, into the obstacles, or sailing faster into the success that awaited us. Not knowing made cowards of us all, put the child back into our faces, the tension back into our eyes, lowered our voices, quickened our smiles, sped our tender hearts.

For Chandler and me, there was an added reality. Time wasn't just ticking on our childhood, it was ticking on our budding romance. He was scheduled to leave for an early orientation and had decided to start with some summer courses. Despite all of our urgent and firm pronouncements of love for each other, we couldn't help but wonder and be anxious about the days of separation, the great distances between us, the direction our new lives would take. It shadowed our every move, every word, every phone call, every embrace and kiss.

On the Thursday before graduation ceremonies, the phone rang just before noon. Mommy answered and called me with a cry that at first frightened me. What new terrible event had occurred? My first thought ran to Chandler and his family, but Mommy wasn't looking gloomy when I bounced down the stairs and turned to her and the phone.

"It's Mr. Wengrow," she said breathlessly. "You've been accepted. He wants to congratulate you."

She held the receiver toward me. For a moment I couldn't move. It was as if I was being handed the torch to carry for so many people, the torch to bring them out of the darkness and into the light Mommy had wished and prayed for so many times.

She shook it impatiently.

I lunged forward, took it, and brought it to my ear.

"Mr. Wengrow?"

"Congratulations, Honey. You beat out some of the country's best. Madame Senetsky was very impressed with you. I hope you understand what a wonderful opportunity this is. Well more than ninety percent of her graduates go on to successful careers and those who don't, don't because of some personal failing, not because of her schooling. You'll be receiving a packet of information in an overnight delivery. I'm very proud of you and proud to have been part of your success. Don't forget me when you become rich and famous," he kidded.

"Oh, I won't, Mr. Wengrow. Thank you. Thank you so much," I cried.

Tears were streaming down my face so hard, I could fill a dry well.

Mommy hugged me and then we went out and hurried to the west field to tell Daddy and Uncle Simon.

"We'll celebrate. All of us. We'll go to a fancy restaurant tonight!" Daddy cried. "We'll spend so much money, Grandad will spin in his grave. Twice!"

Uncle Simon laughed. They both hugged me and I hurried back to call Chandler. He came driving over soon afterward and we went to what had become our favorite place down by the pond.

"I'm very happy for you, Honey. I knew this would happen. I just knew it."

"I didn't. I thought I was not going to get it. They were so impersonal."

"That's the theater. That's the world you're going to be in. It's better if you don't make too much of an emotional investment in your every opportunity. Get used to disappointment, rejection, defeat, and turn your back on it so you can go on."

"You sound so wise sometimes, Chandler."

"I'm just used to disappointments in a different sort of way," he said.

"I hope you'll find what you want out there, Chandler."

"I will," he said. "I've already found it in you."

We kissed and held each other and looked out over the pond. Every once in a while a fish popped up or a frog splashed. The clouds in the distance spread themselves thinner and thinner, revealing more and more blue skies, more and more promise.

"You'll come to New York, won't you?"

"Sure," he said. "When you want me to come."

"I'll always want you to come to see me, Chandler."

He smiled.

"I hope so."

We walked back to the house, holding hands. Mommy invited him to dinner, but he said he had to go to some dinner with his parents. He thanked her.

"Sometimes, I feel so sorry for him," Mommy said afterward. "I hope he'll be happier."

"He will."

"Of course he will," Mommy assured me. "Remember," she whispered, "have faith in the future. Some people are so pessimistic, they miss the wonderful opportunities. They become blinded by their hardships, so blinded they miss their blessings."

"You never did, Mommy."

"The day you were born, I knew I never would," she said.

Epilogue

—◆◆◆—

There was a different light on Graduation Day now. Gone was the sense of an end. It was replaced with a wonderful sense of a new beginning.

Uncle Simon brought a truckload of flowers over to decorate the stage, and the people who attended said it was the most beautifully adorned graduation they had ever seen at our high school.

The band teacher asked me to play a solo piece as part of the program, but I asked if I could do a duet with Chandler instead.

"If he'll do it," he said. He had long ago given up on Chandler doing anything at school performances. However, Chandler agreed, and we performed a Beethoven sonata. The applause was deafening.

When the principal handed us our diplomas, he

announced what our future plans were to be. I saw how impressed everyone was when they learned I was going to a prestigious school of performing arts in New York City.

"We'll hear about this girl soon enough," he declared.

Mommy's eyes were drowning in happy tears, and Daddy and Uncle Simon looked like twins with their matching smiles of pride.

There were a number of parties afterward, one of the biggest and most elegant at Chandler's home. He and I made an appearance there and then left under the excuse of having to attend a few others. His parents didn't seem to mind. They were enjoying their friends. His mother soaked up her role as hostess.

"I thought I was going to suffocate in there," Chandler declared.

We laughed and drove off, but instead of going to another party, we returned to our favorite place on my farm. Chandler had brought a blanket along and we spread it out and lay beside each other, gazing up at the splash of stars.

"I always found it fascinating that people in the same hemisphere, thousands and thousands of miles apart from each other, could look up at the same stars," Chandler said. "You see that group twinkling there, the Seven Sisters?"

"Yes."

"Let's declare them ours tonight, and every time we can see them let's think of each other, forever and ever, no matter where you are or where I am."

"Okay."

"You're going to be a famous person someday, Honey. You're going to do wonderful things."

"What about you? You're just as talented, if not more so, Chandler."

"I don't know. I don't burn with it the way you do when you play. Not yet at least."

"You will."

"Maybe," he said smiling. He kissed me. "I do love you," he said. "I can't imagine falling in love with anyone else as deeply."

"I hope not," I said. "I didn't think you would want to love me. I thought you would become impatient and angry with me because I wanted to wait until... to wait before we..."

"I can't help loving you."

"I know it's different for boys. They don't want to be teased, disappointed."

"I'm not feeling teased, but I'm not saying I'm not anxious about it."

He smiled and ran his fingers down my neck and over my breast, bringing his lips to mine.

"There aren't many girls your age who would stop, who would want it to be so special," he whispered.

"Maybe it's because of the way I was brought up.

Maybe I've got to break free of so many things first. Maybe I've got to stop seeing Grandad in the darkness, making me feel guilty. I can't help being afraid—not of going to hell, but of becoming like him, spending my life hurting people so I would feel less guilty about myself. Does that make any sense?"

"Yes," he said. "Tomorrow, you will start to leave it all behind. I believe in you, Honey, more than I believe in myself."

He put his arm around me so I could cradle my head against his shoulder and we looked up at the stars again. A cloud drifted along, blocking the Seven Sisters.

"Get off there," Chandler cried. "Go on with you."

The cloud moved away.

And we laughed and held each other and filled our hearts with the faith that we could always do that, always blow away the clouds that threatened our stars.

POCKET STAR BOOKS
PROUDLY PRESENTS

FALLING STARS

V.C. ANDREWS®

Available December 2001
from
Pocket Star Books

Turn the page for a preview of
FALLING STARS. . . .

If any of us have ever wondered what it would be like to be in the presence of royalty, we were finding out at this moment, I thought. With a regal air that seemed to precede her and wash over us to make commoners of us all, Madame Senetsky appeared. Ms. Fairchild remained a few feet behind as if it was forbidden to stand too close to her imperial self.

In her left hand, Madame Senetsky held a jeweled cane with a meerschaum handle. She wore a dark suit with an ankle-length skirt. The jacket was open, revealing her pearl silk blouse and prominent bosom. There were strings of pearls around her neck. Her blue-gray hair was pinned tightly in a chignon and fastened with jeweled combs as well. Almost all of her fingers had rings, ranging from simple gold bands to large rubies and diamonds.

She had to be at least in her mid-sixties, yet she had the complexion of a woman far younger. Her skin had an almost silvery tint with only tiny wrinkles around her eyes, but a remarkably smooth forehead.

Elegance and sophistication were defined by such a woman, I thought. She had perfect bone structure, with a very strong, firm mouth, the lips of which were just barely tinted a light crimson. When she drew closer, I saw that her surprisingly youthful appearance owed a great deal to the smart use of makeup. Even so, her blue eyes were youthfully bright, intelligent, gathering information about us in seconds. Between her perfect posture and slow, confident air, we could barely shift our eyes an inch away from her. This was a woman who not only demanded attention, but easily commanded it as well.

She considered each of us, lingering on our faces as if she wanted to be absolutely sure that no impostor had come into this school under false pretenses.

"I am here not only to welcome you today," she began in a voice so careful, so precise, I couldn't help but be impressed and self-conscious about my own. "But to welcome you to hard work, dedication and sacrifice. There is no pretending that isn't required. Here at the Senetsky School, the only illusions we permit are the illusions we create on the stage."

She paused, took a step closer and once again perused each and every one of our faces as if she was looking for some sign of weakness. Ice looked more annoyed and angry than frightened. Cinnamon stared up at her with two unmoving and unflinching eyes, revealing little emotion. Rose looked calm, that soft smile on her lips. Steven shifted his eyes but looked quite unimpressed, even a bit bored, and Howard nodded as if he was hearing exactly what he had expected to hear.

Was I the only one whose heart was pounding? I gazed back at her, holding my breath.

"You are all here because you have proven to possess raw talent. I will have your talents developed and nurtured by the finest teachers in New York City, indeed in all the entertainment world, but I, myself, will be in charge of developing the proper attitudes in you all.

"To do this, from this day forward I will take charge of your everyday life. You will dress, eat, walk, talk as I instruct. You will learn how to hold yourself properly, how to converse properly, how to present yourself properly, for appearance is an essential ingredient in our lives, far more than it is in the lives of ordinary people. Therefore, I will be in judgment of you constantly, even when you are merely crossing from one room to another, spooning soup, or sitting and reading a book.

"We are, in short, always performing, always on one stage or another.

"You will be unhappy a great deal of the time, as anyone under a microscope of criticism would be, but if you have the grit and determination, you will survive and grow into the successful performer a Senetsky graduate becomes."

She pulled her shoulders back even more and gazed down at us all, searching for some sign of defiance, I thought. No one so much as breathed hard.

"Why all this effort? Why this opportunity? I will give you my philosophy, simple and sweet. Along with all the fame, the accolades, the money and prestige comes an enormous amount of responsibility. We are the truly chosen few, given talents for a purpose.

"We fill the lives of ordinary people, brighten their dreary world with meaningful distraction. We show them beauty where they would see none. We help them appreciate their own powers of perception, their own senses and emotions. We are truly the prophets and the clergy showing them what God means for them to worship, to love and to cherish the most in this world.

"If you are unable to meet the tests I give you, you were not meant to be one of us and I will send you on your way.

"Any questions or comments so far?" she asked.

She looked at us to see if anyone would dare utter a word. No one did.

"When I say you must meet my tests, I do not mean only my instructions and requirements for your education. I especially mean not indulging in the degenerative practices so common to people your age these days.

"Consequently," she said, stiffening her posture again and seeming to rise above us even higher, "anyone caught smoking, drinking, or using drugs will be immediately discharged. From this day forward, you represent this school. You are a Senetsky student," she declared, her voice plush with pride, "and that means you bear my name and you live under the shield of my reputation. I will not tolerate the smallest stain on that reputation.

"In short, you are to live like the old-time studio contract players once lived in Hollywood. Everything you do, you do with my permission first. Even your love affairs and your marriages should be planned to help further your careers."

Steven started to laugh.

"You must have more dedication and commitment than nuns and monks," she insisted, her eyes on him, instantly freezing that laugh into a weak smile.

"Ms. Fairchild has your behavior contracts," Madame Senetsky continued.

"Behavior contracts?" Steven whispered loudly.

"After I leave," she continued, eyeing him, "you are all to sit here and read them and then sign them. If you do not want to sign them, please pack your bags and arrange for your departure. I have a number of students on standby."

She softly tapped her cane on the floor and turned to nod at Ms. Fairchild, who shot forward to hand a behavior contract to each of us.

We watched Madame Senetsky leave and then began to read the contract.

There was a curfew for weekday nights and another for weekends.

Any guests had to be approved before they could visit us.

We were never to have any guests in our rooms.

We were solely responsible for the upkeep of our rooms and we were to care for the house as if it was our very own.

Repeated in bold print were the prohibitions against smoking, drinking, and drugs, with the codicil that all the rules applied to our behavior off the property as well as on. In essence, we were simply never off the property. The world had become the Senetsky School of Performing Arts.

"How come we weren't shown all this before we auditioned," Steven Jessie mumbled. "This is worse than living at home."

"You do have a choice," Ms. Fairchild appeared to enjoy telling him. "Don't sign, and leave."

"Thanks," he replied dryly.

"I don't see any problems," Howard said, signing the contract with a flare. "I know what I want and it's not wasting my talent."

Ms. Fairchild didn't nod or smile at him. She took his contract and waited for the rest of us to finish reading the fine print.

Each of us signed the contract and handed it to her.

"Dinner will be served at seven o'clock. You're all dismissed for now," she concluded, pivoted in an almost military style and walked out.

For a moment it was as if all the air around us had become too heavy to breathe.

"I wonder what she does for fun," Steven queried, nodding after Ms. Fairchild.

"Probably pulls wings off flies," Cinnamon said, rising.

"I'm sure it won't be as bad as it sounds," Rose said hopefully. She looked at me and I smiled.

Ice was still staring at the floor.

"Are you all right?" I asked her.

She shook her head.

"I came here to develop my singing ability. I don't know what she's talking about: being the prophets and clergy? I thought I was here just to learn how to sing."

"You don't just sing, Ice," Howard corrected. "If that was all you were here to do, you could do it in the shower. You're a performer. You heard what Madame Senetsky said. We're special people with special gifts."

"I never felt like someone special," Ice said.

We all started out and headed for the stairway.

"I hope I can invite my boyfriend to visit," Rose said.

"If not, you'll just go visit him," Cinnamon said.

"Unless Madame Senetsky disapproves," Howard inserted. "Maybe she'll think your boyfriend is a detriment to your career."

"She has no right to say that," Rose cried.

Howard shrugged. "You just signed an agreement giving her that right."

She looked to me and Cinnamon.

"Did I?"

"Technically, I suppose, we all did," Cinnamon said.

Everyone grew quiet as we continued to walk up the stairway.

"I was wondering why my father agreed to this so quickly," Steven said. "Now I know. He wanted me to be tortured."

We paused at my room. I opened the door and, to my surprise, they all followed me in.

"He must have known what it was going to be like," Steven added, throwing himself into my desk chair. The girls stood inside the doorway with Howard across from them, staring at Steven. "No wonder he wrote that tuition check so fast."

"Wasn't he proud of the fact that you had been chosen?" Rose asked.

"He was proud of the fact that I was out of the house," Steven said. "He's put me in the hands of a monster."

"You don't know how lucky you are. None of you do," Howard said. "But you'll realize it soon enough."

"How did someone so young get so much wisdom so quickly?" Cinnamon asked. Ice smiled but kept her eyes down.

"I've just done my research. I know how important her opinion is, in the theater world especially."

"What about Mr. Senetsky?" I asked.

"He was never part of her career," Howard said. "Besides, he's dead now."

"Oh."

"How did he die?" Rose asked.

"All I know is what is rumored," Howard replied.

"Really?" Cinnamon asked, her eyes narrow with skepticism and a small twist in her lips. "And what exactly is rumored? Howard? Tell us. What else do you just happen to know?"

Howard shrugged. "Supposedly, he committed suicide in this very house years ago. That might be another reason why Madame Senetsky has shut up a portion of the mansion, the parts that remind her of him."

"Why would he commit suicide?" Rose asked. She looked close to tears, worried about the answer.

"I don't know. Business failures, maybe. As I said, it's just a rumor."

"How can suicide be just a rumor?" Rose practically demanded.

"The story was it was a gun accident."

Rose looked like she was about to faint, her face drained so quickly. We all stared at her.

"Rose?" I said. "Are you all right?"

"Oh, you're right to be concerned," Howard said, moving toward her. "We should all be concerned."

"Why?" I demanded, impatient.

"There's a story that his ghost wanders the house, back there, in the locked up places..."

POCKET BOOKS
PROUDLY PRESENTS

THE EXTRAORDINARY NOVEL
THAT HAS CAPTURED MILLIONS
IN ITS SPELL!

FLOWERS IN THE ATTIC

V.C. ANDREWS®

Now available
in mass market from
Pocket Books

Turn the page for a preview of
FLOWERS IN THE ATTIC....

The train lumbered through a dark and starry night, heading toward a distant mountain estate in Virginia. We passed many a sleepy town and village, and scattered farmhouses where golden rectangles of light were the only evidence to show they were there at all. My brother and I didn't want to fall asleep and miss out on anything, and oh, did we have a lot to talk about! Mostly we speculated on that grand, rich house where we would live in splendor, and eat from golden plates, and be served by a butler wearing livery. And I supposed I'd have my own maid to lay out my clothes, draw my bath, brush my hair, and jump when I commanded.

While my brother and I speculated on how we would spend our money, the portly, balding conductor entered our small compartment and gazed admiringly at our mother before he softly spoke: "Mrs. Patterson, in fifteen minutes we'll reach your depot."

Now why was he calling her "Mrs. Patterson"? I wondered. I shot a questioning look at Christopher, who also seemed perplexed by this.

Jolted awake, appearing startled and disoriented, Momma's eyes flew wide open. Her gaze jumped from the conductor, who hovered so close above her, over to Christopher and me, and then she looked down in despair at the sleeping twins. "Yes, thank you," she said to the conductor, who was still watching her with great approval and admiration. "Don't fear, we'll be ready to leave."

"Ma'am," he said, most concerned when he glanced at his pocket watch, "it's three o'clock in the morning. Will someone be there to meet you?"

"It's all right," assured our mother.

"Ma'am, it's very dark out there."

"I could find my way home asleep."

The grandfatherly conductor wasn't satisfied with this. "Lady," he said, "we are letting you and your children off in the middle of nowhere. There's not a house in sight."

To forbid any further questioning, Momma answered in her most arrogant manner, "Someone *is* meeting us." Funny how she could put on that kind of haughty manner like a hat.

It was totally dark when we stepped from the train, and as the conductor had warned, there was not a house in sight. Alone in the night, far from any sign of civilization, we stood and waved good-bye to the conductor on the train steps, holding on by one hand, waving with the other. His expression revealed that he wasn't too happy about leaving "Mrs. Patterson" and her brood of four sleepy children waiting for someone coming in a car. I looked around and saw nothing but a rusty, tin roof supported by four wooden posts, and a rickety green bench.

We were surrounded by fields and meadows. From the deep woods in back of the "depot," something made a weird noise. I jumped and spun about to see what it was, making Christopher laugh. "That was only an owl! Did you think it was a ghost?"

"Now there is to be none of that!" said Momma sharply. "We have to hurry. It's a long, long walk to my home, and we have to reach there before dawn, when the servants get up."

How strange. "Why?" I asked. "And why did that conductor call you Mrs. Patterson?"

"Cathy, I don't have time to explain to you now. We've got to walk fast." She bent to pick up the two heaviest suitcases. Christopher and I were forced to carry the twins, who were too sleepy to walk.

"Momma!" I cried out, when we had moved on a few steps, "the conductor forgot to give us *your* two suitcases!"

"It's all right, Cathy," she said breathlessly, as if the two suitcases she was carrying were enough to tax her strength. "I asked the conductor to take my two bags on to Charlottesville and put them in a locker for me to pick up tomorrow morning."

"Why would you do that?" asked Christopher.

"Well, for one thing, I certainly couldn't handle *four* suitcases, could I? And, for another thing, I want the chance to talk to my father first before he learns about you. And it just wouldn't seem right if I arrived home in the middle of the night after being gone for fifteen years, now would it?"

It sounded reasonable, I guess, for we did have all we could handle. We set off, tagging along behind our mother, over uneven ground, following faint paths between rocks and trees and shrubbery that clawed at our clothes. We trekked a long, long way. Christopher and I became tired, irritable, as the twins grew heavier, and our arms began to ache. We complained, we nagged, we dragged our feet, wanting to sit down and rest. We wanted to be back in our own beds, with our own things—better than here—better than that big old house with servants and grandparents we didn't even know.

"Wake up the twins!" snapped Momma, grown impatient with our complaining. "Stand them on their feet, and force them to walk." Then she mumbled something faint into the collar of her jacket that just barely reached my ears: "Lord knows, they'd better walk outside while they can."

A ripple of apprehension shot down my spine. I glanced at my older brother to see if he'd heard, just as he turned his head to look at me. He smiled. I smiled in return.

Tomorrow, when Momma arrived at a proper time, in a taxi, she would go to the sick grandfather and she'd smile, and she'd speak, and he'd be charmed, won over. Just one look at her lovely face, and just one word from her soft beautiful voice, and he'd hold out his arms, and forgive her for whatever she'd done to make her "fall from grace."

From what she'd already told us, her father was a cantankerous *old* man, for sixty-six did seem like incredibly old age to me. And a man on the verge of death couldn't afford to hold grudges against his sole remaining child, a daughter he'd once loved very much. Then she'd bring us down from the bedroom, and we'd be looking our best, and acting our sweetest selves, and he'd soon see we weren't ugly, or really bad, and nobody, absolutely nobody with a heart could resist loving the twins. And just wait until Grandfather learned how smart Christopher was!

The air was cool and sharply pungent. Though Momma called this hill country, those shadowy, high forms in the distance looked like mountains to me. I stared up at the sky. Why did it seem to be looking down at me with pity, making me feel ant-sized, overwhelmed, completely insignificant? It was too big, that sky, too beautiful, and it filled me with a strange sense of foreboding.

We came at last upon a cluster of large and very fine homes, nestled on a steep hillside. Stealthily, we approached the largest and, by far, the grandest of all the sleeping mountain homes.

We circled that enormous house, almost on tiptoes. At the back door, an old lady let us in. She must have been waiting, and seen us coming, for she opened that door so readily we didn't even have to knock. Just like thieves in the night, we stole silently inside. Not a word did she speak to welcome us. Could this be one of the servants? I wondered.

Immediately we were inside the dark house, and she hustled us up a steep and narrow back staircase, not allowing us one second to pause and take a look around the grand rooms we only glimpsed in our swift passage. She led us down many halls, past many closed doors, and finally we came to an end room, where she swung open a door and gestured us inside. It was a relief to have our long night journey over, and be in a large bedroom where a single lamp was lit. The old woman turned to look us over as she closed the heavy door to the hall and leaned against it.

She spoke, and I was jolted. "Just as you said, Corrine. Your children are beautiful."

There she was, paying us a compliment that should warm our hearts—but it chilled mine. Her voice was cold and uncaring, as if we were without ears to hear, and without minds to comprehend her displeasure, despite her flattery.

"But are you sure they are intelligent? Do they have some invisible afflictions not apparent to the eyes?"

"None!" cried our mother, taking offense, as did I. "My children are perfect, as you can plainly see, physically and mentally!" She glared at that old woman in gray before she squatted down on her heels and began to undress Carrie, who was nodding on her feet. I knelt before Cory and unbuttoned his small blue jacket, as Christopher lifted one of the suitcases up on one of the big beds. He opened it and took out two pairs of small yellow pajamas with feet.

Furtively, as I helped Cory off with his clothes and into his yellow pajamas, I studied that tall, big woman, who was, I presumed, our grandmother.

Her nose was an eagle's beak, her shoulders were wide, and her mouth was like a thin, crooked knife slash. Her dress, of gray taffeta, had a diamond brooch at the throat of a high, severe neckline. Nothing about her appeared soft or yielding; even her bosom looked like twin hills of concrete. There would be no funning with her, as we had played with our mother and father.

I didn't like her. I wanted to go home. My lips quivered.

How could such a woman as this make someone as lovely and sweet as our mother? From whom had our mother inherited her beauty, her gaiety? I shivered, and tried to forbid those tears that welled in my eyes. Momma had prepared us in advance for an unloving, uncaring, unrelenting grandfather—but the grandmother who had arranged for our coming—she came as a harsh, astonishing surprise. I blinked back my tears. But to reassure me, there was our mother smiling warmly as she lifted a pajamaed Cory into one of the big beds, and then she put Carrie in beside him. Oh, how they did look sweet, lying there, like big, rosy-cheeked dolls. Momma leaned over the twins and pressed kisses on their flushed cheeks, and her hand tenderly brushed back the curls on their foreheads. "Good night, my darlings," she whispered in the loving voice we knew so well.

The twins didn't hear. Already they were deeply asleep.

However, standing firmly as a rooted tree, the grandmother was obviously displeased as she gazed upon the twins in one bed, then over to where Christopher and I were huddled close together. We were tired, and half-supporting each other. Strong disapproval glinted in her gray-stone eyes; Momma seemed to understand, although I did not. Momma's face flushed as the grandmother said, "Your two older children cannot sleep in one bed!"

"They're only children," Momma flared back with unusual fire. "You have a nasty, suspicious mind! Christopher and Cathy are innocent!"

"Innocent?" she snapped back, her mean look so sharp it could cut and draw blood. "That is exactly what your father and I always presumed about you and your half-uncle!"

"If you think like that, then give them separate rooms and separate beds."

"That is impossible," the grandmother said. "This is the only bedroom with its own adjoining bath, and where my husband won't hear them walking overhead, or flushing the toilet. If they are separated, and scattered about all over upstairs, he will hear their voices, or their noise, or the servants will. This is the only safe room."

Safe room? We were going to sleep, all of us, in only one room? In a grand, rich house with twenty, thirty, forty rooms, we were going to stay in one room? Even so, now that I gave it more thought, I didn't want to be in a room alone in this mammoth house.

"Put the two girls in one bed, and the two boys in the other," the grandmother ordered.

Momma lifted Cory and put him in the remaining double bed, thus, casually establishing the way it was to be from then on.

The old woman turned her hard gaze on me, then on Christopher. "Now hear this," she began like a drill sergeant, "it will be up to you two older children to keep the younger ones quiet. Keep this always in your minds: if your grandfather learns you are up here, then he will throw all of you out without one red penny—*after* he has severely punished you for being alive! You will not yell, or cry, or run about to pound on the ceilings below. When your mother and I leave this room tonight, I will close and lock the door behind me. Until the day your grandfather dies, you are here, but you don't really exist."

Oh, God! This couldn't be true! She was lying, wasn't she? Saying mean things just to scare us. I tried to look at Momma, but she had turned her back and her head was lowered, but her shoulders sagged and quivered as if she were crying.

Panic filled me. . . .

Read all the books in the Orphans series by

V.C. ANDREWS®

Brooke

Butterfly

Crystal

Raven

Runaways

Pocket Books

3005

Read all the books in the Wildflowers series by V.C. Andrews®

Misty

Star

Jade

Cat

Pocket Books